scored

Also by Lauren McLaughlin
Cycler
(Re)cycler

scored

Lauren McLaughlin

random house 🏠 new york

Text copyright © 2011 by Lauren McLaughlin
Jacket art copyright © 2011 by Cliff Nielsen

Visit us on the Web! www.randomhouse.com/teens

Educators and librarians, for a variety of teaching tools, visit us at
www.randomhouse.com/teachers

Library of Congress Cataloging-in-Publication Data
McLaughlin, Lauren.
Scored / by Lauren McLaughlin.–1st ed.
p. cm.
Summary: In the not-so-distant future, teenaged Imani must struggle within a world where a monolithic corporation assigns young people a score that will determine the rest of their lives.
ISBN 978-0-375-86820-7 (trade) – ISBN 978-0-375-96820-4 (lib. bdg.) –
ISBN 978-0-375-89873-0 (ebook)
[1. Science fiction.] I. Title.
PZ7.M2238Sc 2011 [Fic]–dc22 2010028113

Printed in the United States of America

10 9 8 7 6 5 4 3 2 1

First Edition

Random House Children's Books supports the First Amendment
and celebrates the right to read.

For Adelina

scored

1. a gang apart

SOMERTON WAS POOR, but it was also scored, and had been for twenty-one years. It was a trial town, having signed on when Score Corp was still beta testing the software and offering its services for free—including the smart-cams, or "eyeballs," as the kids called them. Shiny black spheres two inches in diameter, they dangled like Christmas ornaments from streetlights and tree branches. They weren't hidden; that wasn't the idea. You were supposed to know they were there, and behave accordingly.

Now the eyeballs watched Imani LeMonde as she walked home from school. It was unseasonably cold for May. The stream of traffic on the Causeway spit icy water at her ankles. Despite the chill, Imani paused for a moment to gaze at her family's marina behind Farnham's Clam Shack. It was the off-season, so only the working boats were moored there—a handful of lobster boats and worn-out tugs clinging to a living in the depleted waters of the North Shore.

Imani's own secondhand whaler was hidden behind Bill Reynolds's tug. A dozen other boats perched on blocks in the lot for her father to tune up in time for opening day. They belonged to the "recreational" boaters—rich guys from other towns who clogged up the river with their sleek, pointless speedboats, and sandbarred with laughable predictability. Imani would have liked to take some pleasure in the dwindling numbers of these yahoos mooring at her marina every season, but with the clam beds in decline and the lobsters growing scarce, those yahoos were the LeMondes' bread and butter.

As Imani walked down the Causeway beneath the dangling eyeballs, she couldn't be sure the software wouldn't discern such uncharitable thoughts. It was unfathomably smart. The eyeballs were not equipped with audio, but the software could read lips, analyze facial expressions, and identify a person based on gait. Just by walking down the Causeway and thinking anything at all, Imani was feeding it the data it required to produce her score. But Imani also wore the cuff, which measured her pulse rate and pinged her location to the software every second of every day, in case she wandered out of the eyeballs' range. The cuff was a gift from Score Corp—her reward for scoring above 80. It was made of a dull black metal that snapped around her wrist and protruded slightly from her sleeve. It had lightning-fast connectivity and free unlimited data. Imani used it in place of a cell. It was one of the things that visibly differentiated the high scorers from the low. Its shiny tap screen was layered with fingerprints, and Imani had a nervous habit of wiping it clean on her pants leg, which she did now, realizing only after the fact that the software would know exactly what to make of the gesture—even if she did not.

When Imani reached the hard-packed sand of Marina Road, the traffic noise of the Causeway gave way to the quiet rustling of marsh reeds. Imani stopped for a moment to savor the sound. There were no eyeballs here. Marina Road was private, owned by her family for four generations.

Imani knew the score existed to help people like her, that without it her prospects would be dim indeed. Jobs were scarce around Somerton, and her family's marina could barely keep them afloat. The score was "the great equalizer," and Imani knew that as a "highbie" she was poised to benefit at the highest level. But she always breathed easier when she arrived at those marsh reeds. They marked the boundary of a separate place, an unwatched territory.

While she gazed upward at the swooping arcs of some seagulls squawking over a disputed find, a mechanical growl intruded on the natural soundscape. Low, insistent, and louder than necessary, it was easily distinguished from the factory-installed hum of other vehicles. This growl was a custom job. Imani stepped back out onto the Causeway and spotted the growl's source rounding the bend by the 7-Eleven.

Frankenscooter.

The thing was a wreck, a death machine, a mutant scooter pieced together from the salvaged parts of broken Hondas—matte black in places, dented chrome in others, all of the welding announcing itself like proud scars. Its motor—also pieced together from scavenged parts—was too powerful for its cobbled-together frame. But the thing could *move,* which was exactly how Imani's best friend, Cady Fazio, liked it.

Cady and Imani should not have been friends. Imani's score was 92. Cady's was 71, and dropping. That put them in different score gangs. But they'd made a pact back in middle school, when they were both 90s, that, no matter what their scores, they'd always stick together. Even though this was a major peer group violation, they'd stuck to it. They practiced all the rituals of avoidance while at school, but privately, they were a gang apart.

Cady neither slowed down nor signaled for the turn onto Marina Road, an infraction caught by the eyeball above the stone elephant at Abruzzi Antiques. Imani could almost picture it shooting the evidence back to Score Corp for a quick lowering of Cady's score.

And, by association, of Imani's.

Cady angled Frankenscooter toward her favorite spot, then sped up and lurched over the hard shoulder of Marina Road, catching air for a moment before fishtailing around Imani in a sandy blur of secondhand leather and beat-up metal.

"I've got the goods," Cady said. "Get on."

Imani obeyed, and Cady drove down the long sandy strip of Marina Road, the growl of the motor growing more ferocious as they gained speed.

It was only on the back of Frankenscooter or at the helm of her boat that Imani felt truly free. With the wind slapping her face, she reveled in the thrill of motion. That her cuff was pinging the speed infraction to the software, which was shaving off fractions of points, was something she could worry about later.

At Imani's slip, they had her boat's motor tilted out of the water so that Cady could examine its innards.

"Please don't break her," Imani said.

Cady laughed, then pushed her stick-straight, wheat-colored hair out of her eyes. Cady was always messing with her hair, tucking it behind her ears or pulling it into a messy ponytail.

In the hair lottery, Imani had wound up with her father's loose Afro, which she kept pulled back in a long braid to avoid fussing. Her fourteen-year-old brother, Isiah, had gotten their mother's auburn waves, which he buzzed to a quarter of an inch, and Imani had inherited her mother's freckles—just a sprinkling over the bridge of her nose.

"There is so much wrong with this motor," Cady said. "No offense to your dad."

Imani's father had built her boat, a salvage job like Cady's scooter. For that reason, they called her Frankenwhaler.

Cady pulled a circuit board out and replaced it with a slightly larger one. Imani knew little about motors. Her father was the mechanic in the family. Cady had learned most of what she knew by tagging alongside him while he worked, handing him tools and running errands until she'd become something like an unpaid helper. When Cady's interest had turned to scooters, she'd moved on to Gray's Auto, assisting the mechanics there in exchange for free parts. Bartering of that sort was common in Somerton. Spare cash was less so.

"You doing the traps today?" Cady asked.

"If you ever manage to put my motor back together."

Mr. LeMonde's pickup truck pulled into the lot.

"You should begin thinking of ways to thank me for this," Cady said with a cocky smile.

Imani had already been thinking of it. She was going to give Cady the catch of the day if the new motor worked out.

Imani's father got out of the truck and waved to her and Cady, then, unable to resist another mechanic's work, came over to inspect. "You are aware there's a speed limit," he said. "Right, Miss Fazio?"

Cady kept her nose in the motor. "Not on open water, there isn't."

Joining them on the dock, Mr. LeMonde crouched down for a closer look, his dark brown hands so spotted with oil they looked like camouflage. Imani's father and Cady spoke a private language of circuit boards and electronics, of timers and transmissions, all of which were well outside of Imani's core strengths. According to the testing done by Score Corp when she was eight years old, Imani was not mechanically inclined. Her strengths were elsewhere: in the humanities and pure science. Imani had no doubt that the software was smarter than her, but she had no intention of pursuing the humanities. She got enough of that particular species in school. She preferred fish and crustaceans and had long ago decided on a career in marine biology.

When Cady finished her tinkering, Imani dropped the

motor back in the water, waited for Cady to take her place at the bow, then shoved off. Imani could feel the difference in the motor immediately. It was livelier and even sounded different—like a gasoline motor from old movies.

"Don't go crazy out there," her father called as they reversed out of the slip. "Mind the shallows."

"I know the shallows," Imani called back.

She took it nice and slow out of the marina and into the mouth of the Somerton River. When they passed Farnham's Clam Shack, an elderly couple sharing a clam plate waved from behind the seagull-stained window. The girls waved back. Once they were clear of the couple, and seeing no other boats, Imani put the motor to the test. In no time at all, it shot straight up to forty miles per hour, which had been the absolute limit before. Imani pushed it further, and before long, they were doing forty-seven, then forty-eight, which, in the confines of the river, with the tide going out and the mud banks looming on either side, felt like sixty.

Cady sat at the bow with the wind in her face, and when she turned to look at Imani for confirmation of her talent, her hair wrapped around her like a squid's tentacles. She always forgot to bring a hair band, and Imani always kept an extra one in her coat pocket, which she handed to Cady now.

"The lobsters are yours!" Imani shouted over the motor.

Cady smiled with the confidence she wore so well. "It's a pleasure doing business with you, Imani LeMonde!"

"Back at you!"

They entered the narrows around the back of Goodwell's

Fish House, and Imani slowed but continued to go faster than usual. The motor seemed happiest at forty-five—and what a noise! Ancient and analog, it sounded mechanical rather than electronic. Imani loved it!

They emerged from the narrows, and Imani opened the motor up again. There was a little bit of chop to the water, and every time they caught air, Cady squealed with delight. Imani banked and turned, threw the boat in reverse, and did a couple of doughnuts—just to give the new motor a workout before starting in on the traps.

Imani's father kept the lobster commissioner's boat in top shape year-round, and as payment the LeMondes got to keep three traps in the river, free of charge. Checking them was Imani's responsibility. She'd been doing it since she was eleven. If things had ever gotten truly dire at the marina—which was always a threat—she felt certain she could feed her family on what she trapped, caught, and dug up. With most of the commercial enterprises gone, there was little competition for what was left.

The first two traps were empty, so Imani steered Frankenwhaler to Corona Point, a rocky cliff face battered by the turbulent waters of the channel. Imani kept the trap just outside the mouth, where it was safe from the rookie boaters who always underestimated the power of those currents. Rounding the trap, she put the boat in reverse and pulled up right alongside it. Cady reached over and hauled the trap up out of the water two-handed, just like Imani had taught her.

Imani always let Cady handle the lobsters because Cady

was so proud of the way she'd overcome her fear of them. There was a time when Cady hyperventilated just *watching* Imani handle the lobsters. To Imani, this was proof that you could override even the most primal of instincts if you tried hard enough.

Cady banded the lobsters expertly, stowed them in the cooler, then lay back and spread her arms along the edge of the boat. "I feel like we should be drinking a beer," she said. "Isn't that what lobstermen do?"

"Yup. Drink beer, swear, and complain about their wives. Want to anchor and float for a while?"

Cady squinted into the steel-blue water glimmering in the afternoon sun. "You know me," she said. "I never want to go home. My parents are in permanent bitch mode."

Imani dropped the anchor, then stretched out across from Cady. "It's getting worse, huh?"

Cady shrugged, her eyes tracing the progress of a sailboat in the distance.

As sophomores, Imani and Cady had mapped out their futures together. They were still both 90s then, which meant Score Corp would cover tuition at any Massachusetts state school. Cady was going to study engineering while Imani pursued marine biology. Imani's goal was to work for the Fish and Wildlife Department, restoring the local fisheries and clam beds. In her most unencumbered dreams, she envisioned running a fleet of boats with Cady as her engineer in chief (with the caveat that Cady could design state-of-the-art scooters on the side, of course).

"My mom's *obsessed* with college," Cady said. "But she didn't go, so what's the big deal if I don't?"

Imani knew that Cady's mother, who sold handmade clay pots at craft fairs, would have sold a lung to go to art school. But in those days, after the Second Depression wiped out so many universities, higher education became the province of the rich, as it had been originally. It was Score Corp that had reopened those doors for people like Cady and Imani.

"Yeah, but the thing is," Imani said, "it's hard to even get a decent *job* without a good score. I heard the police force just upped their minimum to eighty-five."

"Like I'd want to be a cop?"

"I'm just saying."

"I'll go work for your dad," Cady said. "He'd hire me, right?"

"Yeah. Because business is really booming at LeMonde Marina. So much so, in fact, that Dad was just talking about opening a side business in scooter repair and modification."

"Perfect," Cady said without a hitch. "Then I'm all set." She watched the sailboat making its slow progress near the horizon.

Imani couldn't tell if Cady's blasé attitude toward the future was genuine or defensive. With jobs scarce and the score growing more ubiquitous all the time, businesses could be choosy. Why hire a 71 like Cady when you could hold out for an 89—a bona fide highbie just one life-altering point below the scholarship line.

"You should at least take a break from Gray's Auto," Imani said. "You've been spending a lot of time there, and their kids are unscored. Doesn't one of them actually work there?"

Cady nodded and turned her gaze to the channel, whose

southern shore frothed against the algae-stained rocks of Corona Point.

"Parker Gray, right?" Imani prompted. "I think he was in my gym class last year. Blond hair? Crooked teeth?"

"His teeth are fine."

"That's not the point. By working there, you're associating with him. Maybe that's why your score keeps dropping."

"So what am I supposed to do? Pretend he doesn't exist? Pretend he's invisible?"

"Yes," Imani said. "They *are* invisible. That's what being unscored means. Can't you barter for parts at some other auto shop?"

A look of apprehension flickered across Cady's face, which she attempted to hide by squinting into the sun. "Maybe," she said, her tone dropping, a signal that they should change the subject.

Imani could have pushed, but they had agreed long ago to banish score talk from the river, a ban they usually obeyed. Score talk had a tendency to creep in, especially now, with only a few months left of senior year and their final scores looming.

Imani took a deep breath of salty air and made a determined effort to realign her thoughts. There at the mouth of the channel, beneath the towering cliff face of Corona Point, the world was putting on a brilliant show. Seagulls were diving and the salt air was sticking to her skin. There was not an eyeball in sight, and though her cuff was constantly pinging her location to Score Corp, it was neither score negative nor score positive to be where she was. On the high plateau of Corona Point, the stone facade of one of the mansions was just visible between two pine trees.

There were around twenty mansions on Corona Point. The whole area was private and gated. None of the kids went to Somerton High, and none of the parents kept their boats at LeMonde Marina. They kept them in Waverly, so that they wouldn't have to rub elbows with the few remaining clammers and lobstermen in the area.

Cady followed Imani's gaze up the cliff face to the plateau. "None of *them* are scored," she said.

"They don't have to be," Imani said. "They can buy admission to any college in the world."

"What a racket."

"You sound like my dad," Imani said. She knew such inequities existed, but she also knew that before long the score would be universal. That was what everyone was saying. When that happened, *if* that happened, it wouldn't matter how rich you were. If you didn't have a score, you wouldn't get anywhere in life. You'd be just as doomed as the other unscored, like Parker Gray and his ilk.

For a long while, Imani and Cady faced west, where the distant mound of Hogg Island swallowed the sun in a long slow gulp.

"Man, will you look at that sky?" Cady said. "Will you just look at that shit?"

There *was* something magical about it. How the electric blue deepened and turned steely. Eventually, it would redden in a final burst of color before the darkness swallowed it all.

"Hey, Imani?"

"What?"

"I'd understand completely if you wanted to dump me."

"Shut up."

"No, I'm serious. You know you have to consider it. Before it's too late."

"No score talk on the river," Imani said.

"We were *twelve* when we made that pact," Cady reminded her.

Their separate place, their unwatched territory, had been breached, as all things inevitably were, by the score.

It would be dark soon, but that hardly mattered. There were still three hours until low tide, and as long as there was water in the river, Imani could get them home. She could do it blind if she had to.

"Cady," she said after a long pause, "there are two things in this world I will never give up. Not for my score or for anything else."

"*Two* things?"

"Yes."

Cady paused for a moment to think about it, then said, "Oh, right."

That was the hallmark of true friendship: the things you didn't have to say. None of Imani's fellow 90s would know what she was talking about, because they didn't understand her the way Cady did.

The two things Imani would never give up were Cady and the river.

2. first tuesday

SOMERTON HIGH WAS a squat one-story off the Causeway, studded with clumsy additions in mismatched brick. It had begun life as a clam-processing plant, and when it was low tide in the nearby salt marshes, you could smell that past.

Cady dropped Imani off at the front entrance, a metal double door with three concrete steps leading up to it, then drove around to the back to park her scooter. They wouldn't speak or acknowledge each other for the rest of the day.

Everything inside Somerton High was gray—the lockers, the walls, the floors, even the air. Everything, that is, except for the eyeballs, which dangled at ten-foot intervals from the ceiling. It was a dreary place in the best of circumstances, but on the first Tuesday of each month, when new scores were posted, dreary became ominous.

There were 763 kids at Somerton High, and most of them were scared. Beneath the gaze of the eyeballs, they sized each other up, wondering if they were safe in their gangs, if they dared hope for ascension, or if they were about to be demoted. Whatever their behavior had been for the previous four weeks, the monthly reckoning was at hand.

So as to avoid inadvertent contamination, Imani's gang, the senior 90s, had decided not to acknowledge each other on first Tuesdays until the new scores were posted. It had been Anil's idea, but they'd all agreed that it was mature and showed a serious commitment to self-improvement.

Imani passed Anil every morning on the way to her locker. On most days, he'd smile as warmly as he was capable of smiling and offer a few polite words of greeting. But on first Tuesdays, he didn't give her so much as a glance. Anil Hanesh was going places. At 96, he was one point away from ascension to that most exalted gang of all—the high 90s. There were only two high 90s at Somerton High: Chiara Hislop (98) and Alejandro Vidal (97). Anil wanted to be their lunch mate so badly it had come to define him. The last thing he needed was a 92 with an "unfortunate friend" jeopardizing his chances.

Imani constantly told herself not to take such things personally—either on her own behalf or on Cady's. It was nothing but the execution of an agreement she'd gone along with. It was sober, clear-eyed fitness at its best.

The first two classes were write-offs for most students. It was nearly impossible to concentrate on your teacher when the real grade was floating through the ether, shaped like either a bullet or a kiss. Most teachers knew this and didn't bother introducing anything important until after the scores were posted, which was sometime between nine and eleven.

Imani spent first-period Spanish staring emptily at Mr. Malta's smartboard, with its scroll of verbs in their neatly ordered conjugations. She was not paying attention, which was in violation of the fourth element of fitness, diligence, as well as the second element, impulse control. What she should have been doing was role modeling Chiara Hislop, who sat two desks over.

Chiara was undistracted as she watched the smartboard, her face a picture of serenity. She wore the gold-rimmed data specs given by Score Corp to those who scored 97 or above. The specs provided optical Web access and allowed Score Corp to spy even more intimately on its highest scorers. Imani still had her specs from that one glorious month in eighth grade when she'd crept up to 97. When she'd dropped back to 96 four weeks later, Score Corp had deactivated them. They sat in her sock drawer at home.

Chiara was going to Harvard in the fall, on a full scholarship, provided she maintained her high score. Score Corp would have paid for her to attend any state school in Massachusetts, but Harvard had a special fund for high 90s. Chiara was a true scored success story, having risen from a low of 40 to 98 in four years. Her parents, long ago laid off by the last remaining fish-packing plant in Somerton, had sold her story to a writer in New York. As long as she didn't screw up between now and June, Chiara Hislop, the pride of Somerton, would become a role model for thousands, perhaps millions.

Above Mr. Malta's head, the clock inched forward as the class grew restless. Imani was not the only one committing impulse control and diligence violations. Waves of anxious distraction—the *snick* of tapping feet, the fabric scrape of fidgets— crept from the back of the room. When the bell finally rang, the class leapt, almost as one, for the door. Only Chiara remained calm, gathering her books before walking with extreme compo- sure to the hallway. Imani tried to mimic Chiara's demeanor and pace but soon found her feet rushing forward in the swiftly moving current of Somerton High's lesser students.

To combat cheating and distraction, all mobile hookups—cuffs, specs, cells, tablets, smart scrolls, gloves, etc.—were automatically deactivated on school property by sensors located throughout. The only way to learn your new score was to go online at one of the library tablets or check outside the principal's office, where Mrs. Bronson, the school secretary, taped an alphabetized list up to the glass. A desperate crowd bulged at each location, but to no avail. The scores weren't posted yet. Mrs. Bronson shooed everyone away but wouldn't say when the scores would be up because she didn't know—something she had to remind them of every single month.

Imani's next class was twenty-first-century American history. The teacher, Mr. Carol, was frequently annoying and painfully unfunny, but it was still the most interesting of her classes and, therefore, the *least* conducive to impulse control and diligence violations. In Imani's opinion, however, it should have been renamed Mr. Carol Lectures Everybody about How Dumb They Are for Not Realizing How Dumb Things Have Gotten in This Dumb Country.

Mr. Carol was a "creeper," someone who worried about the "creep" of surveillance and scoring into all areas of society. Like all creepers, he was fond of the phrase "slippery slope," which, regardless of its grim intent, had always sounded nursery-rhyme-ish to Imani. Mr. Carol had tenure, so he couldn't be fired for his beliefs, but rumor had it that the principal, Ms. Wheeler, was dying for him to hug a student or download porn to his smartboard so that she could oust him. Once, Mr. Carol had obstructed the eyeball in his classroom by draping a miniature American flag over its lens. When Ms. Wheeler found out, he had to take it down, then apologize to his students for keeping them out of coverage. It was embarrassing for everyone.

Under normal circumstances, only unscored students, of whom there were thirty-six at Somerton High, were assigned to Mr. Carol's classes. But that year a round of layoffs had left the school one history teacher short, so Imani and two other scored kids had been assigned to Mr. Carol's class.

Imani pitied the unscored. Though some of them attempted to dignify their status with caustic politics, Imani was convinced that was purely defensive. Most of them, she assumed, were the victims of bad parenting. In some cases, their parents had been too lazy, too drunk, or too absent to sign the consent forms. In the absence of a score, the software assumed the worst, which made association with the unscored the severest peer group violation of all.

It was a small class. By senior year, most of the unscored had dropped out of school. Mr. Carol kept the desks in a circle to "encourage free-spirited debate," but this merely resulted in the three scored in the class—Clarissa Taylor (74), Logan Weisgarten (93), and Imani—sitting on one side, while the four unscored sat on the other. Every day, the halves of the circle inched farther apart until Mr. Carol noticed and pushed them back together, reminding his students that classroom interaction was "score neutral." He always used finger quotes when he said it.

Imani took her usual seat between Clarissa and her fellow 90 Logan, being careful to obey Anil Hanesh's first-Tuesday rule. Logan ignored her expertly.

Mr. Carol arrived late and, as he did on most mornings, said, "Good evening." No one had ever laughed at this joke, but that didn't stop him. Mr. Carol carried a banged-up second-hand smart scroll plastered with political stickers, along with a sloppy stack of handouts he'd printed from "the great hive mind of the Web"—another of his un-laughed-at jokes.

"The curriculum Nazis tell me I have to give you guys more tests, so . . ." He glanced around the classroom. "Diego, think of five questions to ask your fellow students about the Second Depression."

Diego Landis, one of the unscored, nodded, then started scribbling in his notebook. Even for an unscored, Diego was strange. He had arrived at Somerton High late in his junior year. Imani didn't know where he'd come from. He had straight black hair, which always obstructed half his face, leaving only one of his blue eyes visible.

Mr. Carol sat on the desk that divided the circle. "Okay, who here knows about the Otis Institute?"

No one did.

"Right," he said. "So Sigmund Otis was this eccentric educator who founded a think tank to—"

"Mr. Carol?" Clarissa raised her hand as she spoke. They were allowed to interrupt, because Mr. Carol believed in treating students as equals. "Should we be taking notes, or is this another one of your . . . you know . . ."

"One of my tangents?" he said. "No. The Otis Institute has this brand-new scholarship. It's for public school seniors only, and they're judging it based on an essay. It's for forty thousand dollars."

"Forty *thousand* dollars?" Clarissa exclaimed. At 74, she was well below Score Corp's scholarship line.

"I know," Mr. Carol said. "And it's renewable every year as long as you maintain, I think it's a B average."

From the way Clarissa's shoulders straightened, it was clear that Mr. Carol's words had opened a window of hope. Clarissa was a good student but had not managed to budge above 74 all year. It was one of the mysterious quirks of the score that dropping was easy but rising was hard.

"So here's what I'm thinking," Mr. Carol continued. "Final paper, I want you all to write an essay for the Otis Scholarship.

Two birds. One stone. What do you think?" Mr. Carol didn't merely assign homework. He proposed it.

"Is this supposed to be a joke?" Rachel Sloane asked. She was unscored, with spiky orange hair and a fondness for snarky comments.

"Of course not," Mr. Carol said.

"So they'll actually give the scholarship to an *unscored*?"

"Only if you write the best essay," he replied.

Rachel folded her arms across her chest. "I don't buy it."

"Look," Mr. Carol said. "Believe me, I know how scarce scholarships are these days, but this one's legit. And the best thing is, it's brand-new. Hardly anyone knows about it yet. I wouldn't be the least bit surprised if one of you won it." Mr. Carol could not prevent his eyes from flicking to Diego Landis.

"Mr. Carol," Logan said. "Do you really think it's fair to hand out a scholarship to someone just for writing one good essay? Some of us have been working hard all of our lives to get over Score Corp's scholarship line."

"You want a medal for being a score whore?" Rachel asked. She managed to shoehorn that phrase into most class discussions.

Next to her, Diego, who'd been writing out test questions for the rest of the class, raised a finger.

"Yes, Diego," Mr. Carol said.

Diego took his time finishing what he was writing, then looked up through his hair. "Correct me if I'm wrong," he said, "but wouldn't it brilliantly upend everyone's stereotype of the unscored as stupid, shiftless deviants if one of us won?" He cast a sly smile at Rachel, who saw his point and took a moment to relish the possibility. "And as to your comment, Logan," Diego continued, "if you think fairness has anything to do with the fact that *you're* getting a full boat to college, then you are seriously deluded."

Logan gazed out the window. "Sour grapes, if you ask me."

"I don't recall anyone asking you," Diego responded.

"Mr. Carol." It fell to Imani to interrupt the debate. Diego would decimate Logan. He always did. And she was in no mood for another display of his showy intellect. Besides, if Logan wasn't careful, his antagonism of the unscored would hurt his score, and by association, hers. "Does this mean you're assuming the unscored have a better shot at winning the scholarship?" she asked.

"Of course not, Imani."

"So it's not rigged?" she asked. "It's not a creeper organization or anything?"

Mr. Carol shook his head vigorously. "The Otis Institute's sole mission is to provide educational opportunities for kids 'overlooked' by the current system." He used finger quotes again.

"Because it would be incredibly unfair," Imani said, "and probably career-damaging for you to mislead us on such a thing." Imani was thinking of Clarissa.

"Imani LeMonde, you are full of suspicion and mistrust," Mr. Carol said. "I like it. Keep it up. Okay, so here's what I'm thinking: five thousand words, and—"

"Five *thousand* words?" Clarissa echoed.

"Yes," Mr. Carol said. "Five thousand whole words. Plus

footnotes. I'm teaching this as a college-level class, in case you hadn't noticed. And in college you don't take multiple-choice tests. They're the height of stupidity, actually. Diego, how are you coming with those questions?"

"I have three," he said. "I need two more."

"Good. Don't go easy on them either. Where was I?"

"The height of stupidity," Logan said in a wounded monotone.

"Right," Mr. Carol said. "Exactly. So, guys, this is your chance to take everything you've learned in class and own it." He squeezed his right hand into a fist. "It's your chance to shine. Okay? So think big. I want to see this thing sourced to within an inch of its life. I want breadth *and* depth. And I want counterarguments too. Don't make it easy on yourself. Engage the opposite point of view. Oh, and feel free to collaborate with your classmates. You guys could learn a lot from each other."

Imani could feel a collective squirm rise up from the seven students.

"Can we write about anything we want?" Clarissa asked. "Like the Second Depression or ..."

"No, no." He shook his head. "Any American high school student can write about the Second Depression. I want to do something that will really stand out. I've given this a lot of thought and ..." He smiled deviously. "I know it's a little out there, but ..."

Imani sensed the arrival of another reckless idea, another career-threatening attempt to "subvert the dominant paradigm."

"What I want," he said, "is for the scored to write essays in *opposition* to the score."

"What?" Logan said. "You can't make us do that."

"Yes, I can."

"Mr. Carol," Clarissa said, "I think I have to be excused from this paper on the grounds that it could totally hurt my score."

"No, it couldn't," Mr. Carol said.

"Yes, it could," Clarissa insisted. "Because actually? There was a girl in my health class who asked to be excused from the reproductive system, because impulse control was a fitness challenge for her."

"What does that have to do with anything?"

"And Mr. Concini couldn't count that section in her grade."

"Mr. Carol," Imani said. "I have to agree with Clarissa. Asking us to disparage the score would be endangering us and also—"

"Not true," Diego interrupted.

"Excuse me," Imani said. She looked directly at him, which she usually avoided. "I was speaking."

Diego stared back with his blue eye, unintimidated.

Regaining her composure, Imani turned away and faced Mr. Carol. "Anyway, it could also get you in trouble. You know like when you did that thing with the flag and the eyeball?"

"Why, thank you, Imani," Mr. Carol said. "I do appreciate your concern. But you're off the mark here." He wagged his finger at her. "And something tells me you know that. Score Corp does not punish academic inquiry. It's"—out came the finger quotes—" 'score-pos.' "

"Exactly," Diego said.

"What would you know?" Logan asked without looking at him.

"More than you," Diego said. "Most of the scored are completely ignorant about their own system."

"*You're* ignorant," Logan tossed back.

"Well argued," Diego replied.

"All right, all right," Mr. Carol said. "Look, people, I can't force you to write about any particular topic for the Otis Scholarship. If you want to write about the Second Depression or the Federalist Papers or any other run-of-the-mill topic, go for it. But for *this* class, the final paper will be what I say it is. I have tenure, so I can do that sort of thing. And incidentally, I happen to know a few people on the board at Otis, and I happen to know that they are very, shall we say, *open* to nontraditional thinking. Let's just leave it at that, okay?"

"Are you saying you have inside information?" Imani asked.

"Only what I've just told you. And no, I'm not on the board, so don't get all conspiracy theory on me or anything. Now, while the scored are writing in opposition to the score, I want the unscored to take up its defense. Its *rigorous* defense."

"Oh, you've *got* to be kidding," Rachel said.

Diego laughed quietly. "That's brilliant."

Rachel turned on him, eyes flashing. "Are you insane?" she said. "How are we supposed to *defend* the score? It's blatantly discriminatory."

"Well," Mr. Carol said, "that's a great argument for one of your scored classmates to use. Your job, however, is to argue the other side."

"There is no other side," she said.

"There's always another side," Diego said.

"Thank you," Mr. Carol said. "I'm glad someone appreciates my vision. How are you coming with those questions?"

Diego ripped a page from his notebook and handed it to him.

Mr. Carol read it while nodding approvingly. "Interesting," he said. "Very interesting."

Diego sat back and glanced smugly around the room. Only one of his eyes was visible through his hair, and Imani wouldn't look at him directly, but she could have sworn he was seeking her out.

The scores were posted after American history, and the fallout was immediate. Thessaly Morris was crying into her locker, having obviously fallen sharply from the 90s. She was a junior, though, so there was still time to work her way back up. A couple of freshman boys high-fived each other, having ascended in tandem.

Imani walked past both the library and the principal's office, but the crowds there were so thick and the anxiety so pungent that she kept walking. She dreaded that first moment of discovery, when she found her name on the list and saw the two digits right next to it. Even imagining it sent her stomach into free fall. She preferred waiting for her gang to tell her at lunch. At least that way she wasn't alone with the news.

She was one of the last stragglers into the lunchroom, and instead of going directly to her table of senior 90s, she hung back and watched her fellow students reconfigure themselves. There were no outbursts, no tearful good-byes. By the end of the year, even the freshmen knew the drill. You went where the score sheet told you to go. You introduced yourself to your new gang, and you sat down. Whatever pain you felt about leaving your former gang behind, you buried it. Whatever jealousy you felt toward the ones ascending, you buried that too. The only tables that never changed were the unscored tables all the way in the back by the teachers' lounge. Sometimes Imani envied them.

She noticed right away that Anil Hanesh was missing from her gang's table. Scanning the lunchroom, she spotted him sitting with Chiara Hislop and Alejandro Vidal. His hard work had paid off. In a few days, he'd receive his specs from Score Corp and a handful of letters from Ivy League schools, welcoming him, at their expense, to the ranks of the superelite, pending the maintenance of his high score.

Imani knew she would never speak to him again. *Good-bye, Anil,* she thought. *It was nice never knowing you.* Imani didn't see Cady anywhere, but Cady often spent lunch period alone in the courtyard rather than with her gang. She felt no bond with the 70s, and they were happy to ignore her, assuming, perhaps, that she'd continue to drop.

As Imani walked to the table of senior 90s where she'd eaten lunch for the past year, Annabelle Kropski's mouth dropped open. Jason Friberg and Itziar Gomez started whispering to each other, and Logan stared at her in surprise before recovering and looking away.

"What?" Imani said. "What happened?"

Annabelle got up and left. The others stayed but refused to face her. Imani found herself staring at the back of Logan's head.

There was only one explanation for their behavior.

"Don't make a scene," Logan whispered, without moving. "Do the right thing, Imani."

It took what seemed like an hour but could only have been seconds to realize what had happened. By then, as if directed by an outside force, Imani was running from the lunchroom.

The hallways were empty except for a few teachers heading belatedly to the lounge. When Imani arrived at the glassed-in reception area of the principal's office, two underclassmen girls were celebrating their good fortune, unable to pull their eyes from the brand-new digits that represented hope and bright prospects. Imani sidled up to the glass and ran her eyes down the list, a gasp escaping when she found her name.

LeMonde, Imani: 64

"Sixty-four!" she cried.

The two girls backed away, leaving Imani to stare at her name and those two unfathomable numbers. What had she done? What had she *not* done? To fall so far so fast, surely she had to have done *something*. She pressed her face close to the glass and traced the invisible line from her name to her score. There was no mistaking it. She was a 64.

Below the scholarship line. *Far* below.

"I thought if I didn't tell you, it wouldn't hurt your score."

In her shock, Imani didn't recognize the voice. But when

she turned, she saw Cady standing there, eyes red, one hand kneading the other. Imani scrolled down the alphabetical list for "Fazio, Cady." Next to her name was the number 27.

"Oh my God," Imani said.

"I'm so sorry."

"What did you *do?*"

From behind the fake wood countertop of the reception area, Mrs. Bronson spotted them, wasting no time in coming out to order them either to class or to lunch, as this was not "social hour."

"I'm so sorry," Cady said. "I'm so, *so* sorry."

An eyeball above the door captured them loitering. Fractions of points were being shaved off their scores. Imani motioned for Cady to follow her back to the lunchroom.

"Just so you know," Cady said, "I love him."

Imani stopped walking. "What? Who?"

They were at the lunchroom's double doors, and the entire student body seemed to be aware of their presence.

"I thought I could protect you," Cady said, "if I didn't tell you."

"Tell me what, Cady?"

Cady's lip began to quiver. "I love him," she said. "I can't help it. I just—" She turned and ran down the hallway, each eyeball capturing her flight.

3. the 60s

"HERE'S WHAT I heard," Amber Frampton said the next day at lunch. "I heard she slept with Parker Gray *repeatedly* just to get parts for that retardo scooter of hers."

Imani knew that was a lie and that the word "retardo" was both offensive and score negative.

"And then," Amber continued, "they, like, fell in love or whatever. But basically, yeah, she whored herself out for her scooter."

Amber Frampton: 66. Core strengths: congruity and peer group. Core weaknesses: impulse control, diligence, and rapport.

Amber had introduced herself that way when Imani first sat down. Imani was in the 60s now. Her old gang were strangers to her. She'd have to eat lunch with Amber every day. She'd have to endure politely while Amber popped her gum and flicked her red curls over her shoulder, all the while disparaging anyone who wasn't in her gang–the lowbies for being stupid and the highbies for being stuck-up.

It was Wednesday, and Imani had neither seen nor heard from Cady since she'd dropped her bomb. Cady hadn't picked Imani up that morning for school, hadn't driven Imani home the day before, and wasn't answering her cell. Imani pieced the story together from the gossip whipping around the school like rubbish in a windstorm. Already, a cautionary tale was forming about the hazards of proximity to the unscored, with Cady portrayed alternately as hapless victim and shameless slut, and Parker Gray portrayed always as the Evil Unscored Seducer Who'd Ruined Cady Fazio for Good.

"The thing is, Imani, we *are* concerned about your association with Cady Fazio." At 68, Connor Riley was the new leader of the gang, the former leader having ascended to the 70s.

All eight of Imani's new gang members stared at her. Connor, Amber, a cornrowed girl named Jayla, a nerdy-looking kid whose name, she thought, was Deon, and four others she'd never met and never noticed.

"What were you even doing with Cady Fazio in the first place?" Amber asked. "She was, like, *two* gangs below you."

Next to Amber, Deon looked both confused and intrigued by the concept, his open mouth revealing double rows of silver braces.

"We had a pact," Imani said.

"What kind of a pact?" Connor wanted to know.

"A friendship pact."

"But she wasn't in your gang," he said.

"I know," Imani said. "That was the point of the pact."

"Um, Imani," Amber said. "Of the five key elements of fitness, peer group is number one in importance."

"I'm aware," she said.

"So..."

"So we had a *pact*," Imani said, hoping to close the subject.

"Look, Imani," Connor said. "We're happy to have you at our table. It's just that we all hope you make the fit decision."

Translation: dump Cady, get a big score boost, then, through the magic of association, drag them all up in time for graduation.

Connor was working Imani, and she was in no mood to be worked. Her life had fallen apart the previous day. Her whole future had collapsed under the weight of a love she hadn't even known existed.

"I'm going to the library," she said. She looked at Deon as she said it, because he seemed the least anxious to use her for his own advantage. They'd had classes together in the past. He was smart, but morbidly shy.

When Imani got up to leave, Amber shook her head and got straight to the task of critiquing her. Over her shoulder, Imani could see Connor watching her walk away, his eyes narrowed to probelike slits. Imani knew she was a last-ditch opportunity for him to breach 70, but only if she dumped Cady Fazio.

And if Imani didn't dump Cady now, with everything she knew, next month she'd drop even lower.

* * *

When Imani got home from school that day, Cady was pacing the first dock, her hand tracing the rail of Will Delbardo's whaler.

"If you want me to leave, I will," Cady said. "I can ride up to the eyeball at Abruzzi Antiques and tell it that you ordered me off your property."

"It would know you're lying."

"Not if you actually ordered me off your property."

"How long has it been going on?"

Cady sighed. "Are you sure you want to know?"

"I just can't believe you kept this from me."

"I did it to *protect* you."

Frankenscooter was parked next to the smaller of the two boat trailers, and Imani noticed the heavy bags strapped to it. Cady turned to look at them. "Yeah," she said. "They kicked me out."

Cady's parents had been threatening to kick her out for six months, but Imani had never dreamed they'd do it. She could tell Cady was doing her best to keep her expression neutral, but there was need in her eyes. What Imani should have said next was *You can stay with us.*

They had a pact. It was as simple as that. And the pact was not conditional. They were friends, not peers, and what did that even mean if they weren't there for each other in a time of need?

But Imani didn't say those words, or any others, and the sinister pause that sprung up in their absence seemed to come from someplace alien, some newly discovered fold in the fabric of reality. Had it always been there, or was Imani creating it with her silence?

It was Cady who guided them out of it with an attempt at looking on the bright side. "So Parker's aunt has this huge house in Donverse, and she said I can have the spare bedroom if I help her paint."

"No," Imani said, too late. "You can—"

"Really," Cady said, shaking her head. "It's cool. Anyway, I just came over to see how you were."

Imani stalled. She wanted to go back to the moment when she might have asked Cady to stay with her. Or back even further, to the point when she might have stopped Cady from falling in love.

"But what exactly have you and Parker—"

"Imani, the less you know the better."

"I'm just trying to understand."

"Don't," Cady said. "It's better for your score if you don't."

Imani sighed. "But what about you? Twenty-seven is so—"

"Don't worry about me," she said. "Just get back over that line." She fastened her helmet and swung her leg over the scooter. "You're the brainy one. You *have* to go to college." She walked Frankenscooter backward until it was pointed toward Marina Road. "So do whatever it takes, okay? Promise me that?"

Imani could only nod.

"And don't look like that," Cady said. "I'll see you in a month. You'll survive, I promise."

"But—"

"Whatever it takes," Cady said. "I mean it." She didn't wait for an answer. She squeezed the accelerator and growled away, quietly at first, then with growing ferocity. Frankenscooter left a wake in the marsh reeds as she sped down Marina Road. There was a break in the growl as she paused at the end to wait for the traffic on the Causeway to clear. Then she roared off, way above the speed limit, beneath the gaze of every eyeball between there and Donverse.

"It's a real shame, that's what it is," Mr. LeMonde said at dinner that night. "A *damn* shame. Such a nice girl too. And a fine mechanic. A *fine* mechanic."

Her mother had made spaghetti and meatballs, which was Imani's favorite meal. Three meatballs sat uneaten atop the heap of spaghetti Imani had been pushing joylessly around her plate.

Across the table, Imani's fourteen-year-old brother, Isiah, slurped up a long strand of spaghetti and wiped his mouth on the back of his hand. He'd scored 85 the previous day, one point higher than the last month. "What I don't get is why anyone would throw their life away for some—"

"For some what?" Imani interrupted. "For some unscored piece of trash?"

"Yeah," her brother said. "Exactly."

Their mother plopped a pitcher of extra sauce in front of him. "Isiah," she said. "Let's not use language like that."

"She said it. Not me." He poured more sauce on his already dripping spaghetti.

"I was being ironic," Imani said.

"I just think it's a damn shame," their father repeated. "What kind of a job's she going to get with a score like that?"

"Dad," Isiah said. "You're not supposed to swear in front of us."

It was sweltering in the dining room because that was where the wood-burning stove, which they'd had to fire up again because of the cold spell, sat. The rest of the house was varying degrees of cool, tepid, and frigid, but the dining room was tropical. It was inviting and cozy at the beginning of dinner, but about halfway through they ended up stripped down to their T-shirts and grumpy from the heat. That point had already been passed.

"Elon," Imani's mother said, "save the curse words for me."

"Naw, I like to cash those in at the VFW." He winked at his wife. "Sorry, Isiah. I shall speak more proper in the future."

"Proper*ly*," Isiah corrected with an eye roll only a middle schooler could pull off.

Isiah was entering a truly obnoxious phase, but Imani didn't blame him. She blamed middle school. She remembered her time there. A vicious, backstabbing snake pit.

"So, Imani," her mother began in her gentlest voice, "what's the thinking now? Are you still going to be seeing Cady, or . . ."

Her whole family was staring at Imani now.

"I guess you need to do what's right," her father said, breaking the uncomfortable silence. "What's right for you, I mean."

Imani rarely discussed anything score-related with her

parents. They were exactly one generation too old to understand. They might have had their own challenges growing up, like SATs and other standardized tests and something called No Child Left Behind. But they didn't know what it was like to be watched and evaluated *all the time*. Imani's parents had read the brochure and signed the consent back when she was eight years old. They understood the *reasons* for the score. They understood the opportunities it afforded, but they didn't–and couldn't–understand what it was like.

And Imani was in no mood to enlighten them. "I can't eat," she said. She pushed back from the table and ran upstairs to her bedroom.

Wrapping herself up in her grandmother's handmade afghan, Imani sat on the bed and stared through her window at the purpling sky, a bank of covered speedboats hunkering down in the gloom. After a while, she was forced to conclude that her frustration at dinner had nothing to do with her parents. She had no complaints there. They were patient and loving and always did what they thought was best for her. It wasn't their fault they'd grown up in a different world. She'd run upstairs because she couldn't bear to answer their questions. She didn't have the heart to tell them that Cady had already made the decision for her, that Cady had backed away gracefully so that Imani could save herself.

And Imani had let her, which was less a decision than an act of paralysis. She had yet to determine whether this rose to the level of betrayal or if it was the result of a stalwart fitness finally stepping up to do what she should have done long ago. She only knew how it felt: sickening, sinking, like a flu of the mind.

Imani had been rubbing her cuff's tap screen on the afghan until it was buffed to a high gloss. The thing was dead now, already deactivated. She'd worn it one extra day because she couldn't bear the naked feeling of cool air on her wrist. She took it off, noting the indentation on her skin, and placed it in the sock drawer next to the dead specs, trying not to think of them as emblems of her downfall.

Digging around, she found her old cell, something she hadn't used in years. She turned it on, surprised that its battery still held some charge. A few taps and she'd signed on to her family's plan. She could get online, make calls, use the GPS, just as she could with the cuff; and just like the cuff, it would ping her location to Score Corp. In most ways, it was as good as having a cuff. But it meant she was no longer a highbie.

The purple of twilight deepened to black, the covered speedboats dissolving into the background of marsh reeds. Several times, Imani *almost* called Cady, knowing the software would punish her for it. That she didn't, that she remained in a state of indecision about her best friend, was a strange comfort to her. Cady might have made up *her* mind about what was best for Imani, but Imani had yet to make up her own mind.

4. a destiny of worms

EVERY MORNING, IMANI walked with Isiah down Marina Road to wait for the middle school bus. Usually, they'd kick a stone back and forth until it veered off into the marsh reeds, then he'd challenge her to a sprint. For years, Imani had let Isiah win at the last minute, but lately, despite still being eight inches shorter than her, he'd been winning on his own. Isiah was a jock, a star of the middle school hockey team, his dreams of "going pro" just beginning to mature into the more plausible, and therefore more hazardous, ambition of "playing in college."

That Thursday, Isiah walked more quickly than usual and refused to kick the stone Imani passed to him. Near the end of Marina Road, he took a running start, then skidded to a hockey stop on some wet leaves right at the lip of the Causeway.

"Be careful!" Imani yelled.

"Don't talk to me," he said.

The nearest eyeball was above the stone elephant at Abruzzi Antiques, but it couldn't see them. Isiah's coverage began when he boarded the bus. Imani's had always started when Frankenscooter passed the pawnshop on the Causeway.

After a long sulky pause, Isiah said: "You can't seriously be thinking of staying friends with her. She's a lost cause. Everyone knows that."

"Everyone at the middle school?" Imani said. "Really? What other wisdom are they passing around in *eighth grade*?"

"Don't be stupid, Imani. If you let her take you down, you're no better than her."

"Cady never cared that you were below us," Imani reminded him. "She never complained about giving you rides to hockey when Mom and Dad were busy."

"Yeah, well, she wasn't a total slut back then."

That was how it was now. Nobody knew the true details of Cady's relationship with Parker Gray. Imani didn't even know them. All anyone knew was that Cady had squandered her score to date an unscored boy and that made her a slut. End of story. And now, in order to save herself, Imani was expected to join the mob of Cady haters. That was the score-positive choice. It was the fit thing to do.

The bus appeared around the bend by the 7-Eleven, and Isiah stepped away from his sister. "Don't talk to me, okay?"

When the bus stopped across the street and unfurled its blinking red stop sign, he ran for it without even saying good-bye. Imani could see him sit next to his gang buddy, Max, a chubby boy with a mop of curly dark hair. As the bus pulled away, Max narrowed his eyes at Imani through the window.

It was such a middle school reaction, Imani thought, and one that would never pass muster in the more diplomatic, if equally brutal, high school realm. Still, it was as clear a sign as any that Cady's story had seeped into every crevice of Somerton. They were all connected by it, because the score connected them all. Isiah was only two removes from Cady, and he'd suffer for it. He'd suffer for his relationship to *Imani*. At 64, she was below him now. Even family could be a liability.

As Imani watched the bus head down the Causeway with its load of lunchroom warriors, she was consumed by a desire to protect Isiah. He was too young, she thought, to begin the full-scale panic that came to those whose ambitions exceeded their options. But that panic would close in soon enough. At 85, Isiah was in the zone where things became tantalizingly possible, though by no means assured.

Really, Imani thought, you might be better off being a lowbie. Or even an unscored. At least then, you *knew* you were doomed.

Cady and Parker stayed out of school that day. In their absence, the cautionary tale of their liaison (variously seen as coercive, financial, and just plain crazy) blossomed into a full-blown Greek tragedy. Students whispered about it, sharing theories, offering possible explanations. They cast sideways glances at Imani, sometimes in sympathy, sometimes in fear. She was used to being watched by the eyeballs, but now she was under the fierce scrutiny of her peers, and it made her uncomfortable.

It did not, however, make Connor Riley uncomfortable. The leader of her new gang was determined to use the situation to launch himself upward. At lunch that day, he gave Imani an ultimatum. "I hope you understand that it's not just for our sake," he said, "but for yours too. We need to know whether you plan to continue associating with–"

"No." Imani cut him off. "I don't. Cady Fazio is out of my life." Imani was keenly aware of the eyeball dangling above and to the right of Connor, as he was surely aware of the eyeball dangling above and to the left of her. Already, their exchange had the aroma of performance about it. And while Imani wisely avoided milking it for effect, Connor had obviously rehearsed a whole speech about how "forgiving" and even "magnanimous" he and the other 60s were prepared to be regarding Imani's past unfit behavior. In an attempt to get at least some of it on the record, he managed to spit out the words "forgiving" and "magnanimous" with little explanatory context. Imani knew he'd be penalized for it.

When Connor had finished, there was an uncomfortable pause; then Deon spoke, quietly and without ever looking up from his sandwich. "Magnanimous," he said. "Characterized by a lofty and courageous spirit. Showing nobility and generosity of the mind."

The table fell silent for a moment, then Jayla shook her head and joined with Amber in rolling her eyes. Judging from the reactions of the rest of the gang—all variations on the eye roll or the shaken head—Imani got the impression that the quiet outburst was typical behavior for Deon. As Amber might have said, the boy had a severe rapport deficiency. And though Imani's gang was making it clear that she was expected to despise him for it, his actions had precisely the opposite effect on her. As Deon nibbled his sandwich in ratlike mouthfuls, she found herself warming to him.

At study period, Imani rushed to the school library to claim one of the tablets bolted, against theft, to the long wooden table by the window. The bolts were optimistic at best, as the tablets had been out-of-date even when purchased and were insufficient for most media files. But as they constituted the only link to the outside world at school, each one was claimed before the late bell rang.

The tablets were supposed to be used for homework, and since you had to sign in to use them, Score Corp could, and did, track usage. Despite this, lowbies could be relied upon to hack their way around the firewalls into the forbidden realms of porn, which occasionally flickered at the corners of Imani's vision. She knew better than to let curiosity get the better of her, however. Her eyes never wandered from her own tablet's screen. There were eyeballs dangling above, which would have caught that.

Imani wasn't doing homework, but she *was* doing research.

Though Score Corp refused to reveal any information about its scoring algorithm, other than to insist that it got "smarter all the time," scientists had arrived at the five key elements of fitness through reverse engineering. Specifically, they had studied behavioral patterns in risers and droppers. Like most scored, Imani knew the five elements by heart: peer group, impulse control, congruity, diligence, and rapport.

Peer group had been her weakness, but she'd solved that problem by dumping Cady. What she needed to know was whether that would be enough to get her back over the scholarship line. Her fingers flew across the tablet's tap pad, taking her on a journey studded with amazing riser stories and tragic dropper stories, but it all came to a crushing halt when she found this piece of data:

Although there are many cases of scores dropping rapidly, even as much as sixty points in one month, there are very few examples of scores rising suddenly.

Imani had heard of such a discrepancy but had never given it much thought. Her score had wavered between 92 and 97 for years, with no dramatic changes. Now, however, she had one month to rise twenty-six points and wondered if dumping Cady would be enough. As she jumped from site to site in search of an answer more optimistic than the ones she kept finding, her attention was drawn to the library's main desk, where her principal, Ms. Wheeler, stood in quiet discussion with the head librarian.

Ms. Wheeler was a cool and distant figure: young, pale, with short dark hair. She wore thick-rimmed silver specs that looked like the ones Score Corp gave to high 90s, but older, rounder. In assemblies and announcements, Ms. Wheeler often referred to her "open-door policy," but Imani couldn't imagine any students *volunteering* to visit her. Imani never had. There was something intimidating about Ms. Wheeler. Though her words said "Approach me," her demeanor said the opposite. When she finished her conversation with the librarian, she noticed Imani staring at her, nodded coolly, then left.

Feeling desperate rather than bold, Imani decided to test the open-door policy. When she arrived at the reception area, Ms. Wheeler had already disappeared inside her office, and Imani was met by Mrs. Bronson, who seemed to regard her presence there as an intrusion.

"I'm here to see Ms. Wheeler?" Imani said.

"Did she ask for you?"

Imani shook her head, already wondering if she'd imagined the open-door policy. Ms. Wheeler's *actual* door was closed.

Mrs. Bronson poked her head into Ms. Wheeler's office and said something inaudible. Peering around Mrs. Bronson's ample frame, Ms. Wheeler regarded Imani through her specs, thought for a second, then waved her in.

"Make it quick," Mrs. Bronson warned. "She's very busy."

When Imani entered her office, Ms. Wheeler told her to shut the door. "Imani, right?" she confirmed. "Imani LeMonde." Ms. Wheeler unrolled a tap pad across her desk and began typing, her eyes glazing slightly as she read her specs' flickering display. She wore peacock-blue nail polish, which Imani thought unusual for an adult, though from this close, she seemed younger than Imani had previously imagined–late twenties, perhaps. Imani could make nothing of the flashing lights obscuring Ms. Wheeler's hazel eyes but assumed she was accessing her student file–her score, her past scores, her grade point average and disciplinary record.

"Oh, yes," Ms. Wheeler said. "You just took a big hit, score-wise." She looked at Imani with the half-glazed eyes of someone peering through data. It had taken Imani weeks to acquire the skill, back when she'd been blessed with Score Corp's specs. By the time she'd mastered it, they'd been deactivated.

"You were friends with that Fazio girl, weren't you?" Ms. Wheeler asked. "Even though you weren't in the same gang." Imani couldn't pinpoint Ms. Wheeler's expression. It seemed curious and slightly judgmental. "Sit down. Please."

Imani sat in a cream-colored chair facing Ms. Wheeler's desk. Her office was neat, with only a few books lined up on a shelf and papers perfectly stacked on the corner of her desk. A small bud vase with a white carnation sat on the sill of the small window. On the wall to Ms. Wheeler's left was a gilt picture frame containing her final score report.

PATRINA WHEELER: 98.

"Ninety-eight," Imani said. "Wow. So are those…" She pointed toward Ms. Wheeler's specs.

"From Score Corp?" she said. "Yes. I've had them refurbished, of course, but the frames are the originals."

"Cool."

The corners of Ms. Wheeler's mouth turned up while she continued to type, her eyes glazed by the data. When she'd finished what she was typing, she blinked away her display and looked at Imani with a dazzling smile. "It opened up the world for me," she said. "We were a trial town too."

"Really?"

"Wakachee, Florida," she said, leaning back in her cream leather chair. "It made Somerton look like Beverly Hills."

Imani had trouble imagining Ms. Wheeler as a teenager. She seemed so polished. But now that Imani had conjured the image, she couldn't resist fleshing it out with details. She pictured Ms. Wheeler sitting on the hood of a car in her school's parking lot while eyeballs dangled from palm trees and sunburnt asphalt mirage-wavered in the distance. Perhaps Ms. Wheeler had been the Chiara Hislop of Wakachee, Florida.

"So how can I help you, Imani?"

"Um, well," she said. "I was thinking of what you said last week at morning announcements. You know, about how we should see you as an ally, and that you were here to help us, not only academically but—"

"In score-related matters as well," Ms. Wheeler filled in. "Yes. I remember. No one's taken me up on that. You're the first."

Imani couldn't stop thinking about Wakachee, Florida. Why, she puzzled, would Ms. Wheeler go from a broken-down Florida swamp town (she pictured Wakachee this way now, full of mangroves and mosquitoes) to a broken-down Massachusetts clam town (full of marsh reeds and mosquitoes). With a final score of 98, she could have gone anywhere.

"Imani," Ms. Wheeler said. "Can I ask you a personal question?"

Imani detected the hint of a southern accent, something she hadn't noticed before. "Um, sure," she replied.

"I'm just curious. What was it that kept you and Cady together?" Ms. Wheeler's fingers flew across the tap pad as her specs lit up with data unreadable to Imani. "I see that she'd been dropping for a while. Weren't you concerned?"

"I guess," she said. "But you see, we had this–" She stopped herself. Her reasoning, which in the past had seemed so solid, now seemed faulty, even childish.

"Yes?" Ms. Wheeler pressed.

"We had a pact," Imani said flatly.

"A pact?" Ms. Wheeler shook her head in confusion. "What do you mean?"

"That we'd stay friends," Imani said. "No matter what."

"No matter your scores?" Ms. Wheeler's eyes widened.

Imani nodded. It was clear to her that Ms. Wheeler understood the risky nature of her friendship with Cady in a way that Imani's parents never had. Imani's parents thought it was "sweet" and "heartwarming" that the girls stayed faithful to each other while their classmates shifted from gang to gang. How naive they seemed to Imani now.

Ms. Wheeler sighed and leaned back into the thick cushion of her cream-colored chair. "Loyalty. Interesting. You know, people used to think highly of that trait."

People like her parents, Imani thought.

"Of course, now we know better," Ms. Wheeler said. "Loyalty is a trap, Imani. A disempowering bond. People should earn your respect. Every day."

"I've severed all ties with Cady Fazio."

Imani had not intended to sound so defensive.

"Good. That's great." Ms. Wheeler smiled approvingly. "And how are you getting on with your new gang?"

It was only then that Imani noticed the absence of eyeballs in Ms. Wheeler's office. She thought about all the things she could tell her. She could reveal how much she loathed her new gang, or all the mean, unfit thoughts she'd had about Amber Frampton. In the end, however, she opted for diplomacy, because she found that she wanted Ms. Wheeler to like her.

"I'm still getting to know them," she said.

"Of course. It does take time, doesn't it? Now..." Ms. Wheeler resumed typing. "I see you've been accepted to UMass, pending financial ability and, of course, score maintenance. You're planning to major in...marine biology?" Ms. Wheeler stopped typing and peered at Imani through her flashing specs. "Really? *Marine* biology?"

Imani nodded.

"Not just biology?"

"I want to work on the water," Imani said. "I want to help restore the fisheries and clam beds."

"Oh, I see." Ms. Wheeler nodded deeply. "You want to stay in Somerton."

"Definitely."

"You want to stay and make a difference," Ms. Wheeler said. "Good for you. Personally, I couldn't wait to get out of Wakachee. I wanted to see snow."

"That's funny," Imani said. "Everyone around here complains about the snow."

"I know!" Ms. Wheeler laughed. "Well, they should try August in Wakachee. That'll cure 'em." She flashed Imani her dazzling smile. It was infectious, and Imani found herself warming to her principal and wishing she'd exploited the open-door policy earlier. What an opportunity it was to have direct access to a high 90! And Ms. Wheeler was so friendly.

"So let me guess," Ms. Wheeler said. "You're here because you need to get back over the scholarship line, and you want to know if discarding Cady Fazio will do it."

Imani had been smiling along with Ms. Wheeler, but now her smile collapsed as she tripped mentally on the word "discarding." It made Cady sound like a gum wrapper or an apple core.

"It's just that I've been doing some research," Imani said. "And apparently it's much harder to rise quickly than it is to fall quickly."

"Oh, it's not just harder," Ms. Wheeler said. "It's almost impossible."

Imani felt a catch in her throat. When she spoke again, her voice was fragile, almost falsetto. "But why?"

Ms. Wheeler smiled sympathetically. "You see, the software understands human nature much better than we do. It understands how quickly we can destroy ourselves and how long it takes to improve."

"But I didn't even *do* anything. It was Cady who did it, and I didn't even know about it."

Ms. Wheeler sucked in air through her teeth. "Are you beginning to understand how disempowering loyalty can be?"

Imani slumped in her chair. Of course she understood. Peer group was the first element, and she'd been violating it flagrantly. It's not that she hadn't been aware of the risk, but she'd never dreamed Cady would sink so low as to date an unscored. "Then what am I supposed to do?" she asked. "Without that scholarship—" She couldn't even finish the sentence. She dropped her head in her hands.

"Okay." Ms. Wheeler gripped the edge of her desk, then stood up. "There are, of course, many opportunities for the non-college-bound, Imani."

Non-college-bound? The words were like a dagger to Imani's heart. For as long as she could remember, she had planned to go to college. She'd never even considered anything else. Ms. Wheeler regarded her with pity, and Imani sat upright, trying to control her emotions. "I'm sorry," she said.

"It's okay," Ms. Wheeler said. "I didn't mean to upset you, Imani. It's just that I respect your intelligence, and I don't want to sugarcoat things."

Imani realized she was breathing heavily.

"Okay, Imani?"

"Okay."

"The thing is," Ms. Wheeler continued, "you might need to forget about the scholarship line. Now..." She sat down and resumed typing. "Have you thought about the military?"

Imani's stomach lurched. The military had a true open-door policy. They took anyone.

"You're sixty-four now," Ms. Wheeler said. "If you can rise just one point, that qualifies you for officer training."

"I don't want to go to war."

"It's not war, Imani. It's peacekeeping." Ms. Wheeler's tone lightened as if she were describing a bake sale.

"I want to stay in Somerton."

"Fine. So let's talk about seventy," Ms. Wheeler said. "That's six points. It's a bit of a stretch, but it's not out of the question. At seventy you have real options: child care, health services, management training at any number of retail establishments. Not in Somerton, of course. Nobody's hiring here."

"I *really* want to stay in Somerton."

"Imani, what I'm trying to tell you is that you need to reevaluate your options. You're not a ninety anymore. I know this is a difficult adjustment, but you need to face it."

Imani's head spun with the unraveling threads of her life. The only solid notion she could keep in focus was her family's bait shop. It plunked down in the middle of the maelstrom like Dorothy's shack into Oz. Imani worked there with her mother every summer. She didn't mind it for a few hours a day, a few months a year. She knew all the customers by name, knew exactly which bait to sell for which type of fish. But at the end of each shift, she couldn't wait to get out of there. It was cramped, plagued by wood rot and greenheads. Even after she left, it was a good five minutes on the river before she got the smell of bug spray and bait worms out of her nose. She didn't want to spend the rest of her life there, and she'd never thought she'd have to.

"If you really focus," Ms. Wheeler said, "you can get your score back up a bit, get a decent job somewhere, start saving. Who knows. Maybe a few years down the line..." She let the fantasy trail off. Such optimism, she had to know, was beyond Imani's means. College was the destiny of the rich and the 90s. Imani's was a destiny of worms. "There are opportunities for self-improvement everywhere," Ms. Wheeler went on. "You just have to keep your eyes open for them. *Little* opportunities here and there. You'll see."

Imani had no idea what Ms. Wheeler was saying now, but she was afraid to speak up, lest her emotions spill out again.

There was a knock on the door and Mrs. Bronson peeked in. "It's him," she said.

"Okay," Ms. Wheeler said. She waited for Mrs. Bronson to close the door. "I'm going to have to take this call, Imani. Are you going to be okay?"

It was a question too weighty for Imani to answer honestly, so she nodded evasively.

Ms. Wheeler leaned across the desk and took on a conspiratorial tone. "This next month is going to be critical, Imani. Don't let despair get the better of you. Work the five elements. Work them hard." There was a trace of optimism on Ms. Wheeler's face, which Imani clung to like a drowning person.

"Little opportunities," Ms. Wheeler said. "Keep your eyes open for them." She disappeared once again into her specs, lights flashing, peacock fingers flying. "And drop in anytime," she said. "My door is always open."

After school, it was violently sunny. Imani walked home along the Causeway beneath the eyeballs, and when she met the gentle *whish* of her marsh reeds at Marina Road, she breathed in deep and hard. She paused to listen to the distant caw of seagulls, reminding herself that this was her sanctuary, her escape. But it felt different now.

Beyond the marsh reeds, the bait shop waited. It was shuttered for the off-season, but it would open soon enough. Then it would swallow her whole.

And that was her best option.

5. the proposal

THE NEXT MORNING, Isiah snubbed her at the end of Marina Road, followed by a hearty glower from his gang buddy Max as the middle school bus carried them both away. But these insults barely registered. Despite Ms. Wheeler's warning, Imani *had* let despair get the better of her. It was warm finally, but it had rained overnight, forcing her to dodge puddles on her way to school. She made only a halfhearted effort, arriving at her school's entrance with sludged shoes and dampened cuffs that perfectly represented how she felt inside.

While she was at her locker, gathering her books, a crowd of unscored came sauntering down the hallway, laughing and cutting a fat wake among the scored they passed. It seemed to Imani that the unscored loved to take up space that way, reveling in their toxicity. Diego Landis was among them, and at one point he walked backward so that he could whisper something to Rachel. To avoid being sideswiped by him, Imani had to press herself against her open locker. But Diego crashed into her anyway, and, to her great embarrassment, a squeal escaped her lips.

"Sorry," he whispered.

He grabbed Imani's hand to avoid falling, and when he regained his footing and rushed off with the others, her skin tingled as she felt the small piece of paper in her hand. Diego had passed her a note. Worse still, he had *touched* her! Imani hadn't been touched by a boy since Malachi Beene had tried to put his hand up her shirt sophomore year. Now, as then, she could feel the shame blossoming red-hot all over her face. She knew it was unwarranted, because she hadn't done anything wrong. But her eyes shot to the nearest eyeball, and it took a few deep breaths to reassure herself that she wouldn't be punished for it.

It wasn't until she closed her locker that Imani unfolded the piece of paper. In the tiniest handwriting Imani had ever seen were the words:

Sorry for the subterfuge, but I have a proposal to make and this was the only way I could think of that wouldn't compromise your score. I want that scholarship, and I suspect you do too. This makes us competitors, but that doesn't mean we can't help each other. What I'm proposing is a discreet collaboration. If you're not interested, say nothing and do nothing. If you are, meet me at the library tonight at 7.

DL

When Imani looked up from the note, Diego was disappearing around a corner with his friends. The hallways gradually drained as students made their way to homeroom. With the note in her hand, Imani let her eyes drift to the eyeball just above and to the right of her. It didn't have a view of the words on the note itself, and, even if it had, the writing was probably too small for it to read. Still, she felt implicated by it. When the late bell rang, she shoved it in her pocket and rushed to homeroom.

I suspect you do too.

As her teacher, Mrs. Ruskin, took attendance, Imani wondered what Diego could have meant by those words. He didn't know her. Since when did he "suspect" things about her? And why had he chosen *her* rather than Logan or Clarissa?

Did he think she was the smartest in the class?

Or the most likely to stray?

In American history, Diego avoided looking right at Imani. Still, she sensed his awareness of her in the way his blue eye would graze her knee, her shoes. The eyeball above the American flag felt more imposing than ever, and Imani couldn't help but wonder if it detected her nervousness. Did it connect that nervousness with Diego? Did the note itself, folded over twice, leave an indicting mark on her jeans?

Was she being paranoid?

Was paranoia score negative?

If so, which of the five elements did it violate?

Imani dreaded being asked a question by Mr. Carol for fear

of a red-hot blush that would give her away. But Mr. Carol got so worked up by a rant on civil liberties he didn't ask any questions at all. When class was over, he realized he'd forgotten to cover the material they'd be tested on, made another remark about the "curriculum Nazis," and told the class they'd have to "really do some plodding" the following week.

Imani rushed out as quickly as possible.

There was no good reason to feel guilty about Diego's note, she told herself. It represented an inappropriate overture on *his* part, not hers. But the longer it remained in her pocket, the guiltier she felt. She could have thrown it away, and every time she passed a trash can she *meant* to, but something stopped her.

In third-period English, she found herself asking "What would Ms. Wheeler do?"

Imani tried to imagine her principal as a teenager again, receiving Diego's note. She'd unfold it, read it, perhaps pause for a moment to think about it. Then what? Imani pictured her standing in the hallway as everyone rushed to homeroom, an eyeball overhead, Diego disappearing around a corner. When she moved the picture forward, she saw Ms. Wheeler walk purposefully to the eyeball and speak quietly to it. High 90s often spoke to the eyeballs. Imani had seen Chiara Hislop and Alejandro Vidal doing it lots of times. She'd heard that the high 90s viewed the eyeballs as trusted confidants rather than fearsome spies, which was how most people saw them. Imani couldn't imagine precisely what Ms. Wheeler would *say* to the eyeball. But the next part was clear. She would unfold the note for the eyeball to read, then tear it up and toss it into the nearest trash can. Ms. Wheeler would not have felt guilty about receiving it. As a high 90, she would be totally congruent. All of her values would be in sync, the fit course of action always apparent. That was *why* she'd wound up with a final score of 98.

Now Imani regretted not taking this course of action right away. By holding on to the note, she'd turned Diego's offense into her own. She'd have to confess now. It was the only way to salvage the situation. She'd wait until study period, when the hallways were empty. Then she'd march straight up to the nearest eyeball, disclose her congruence violation, and put Diego Landis and his unfit proposal behind her.

"Can we at least *discuss* going to the dance tonight?" Amber's whine was at full throttle.

The rest of the 60s ate their lunches in relative quiet while she and Connor argued about the fitness of dances. Connor was of the opinion that dances, like dating, were a minefield of score peril and, therefore, to be avoided at all costs. But Amber argued that avoiding social interaction was itself unfit. As reference, she shot an unsubtle sideways glance toward Deon, the patron saint of social isolation. Deon either didn't notice or chose not to acknowledge it. Eventually, the others chimed in with their opinions. Imani stayed out of it.

In the far corner of the lunchroom, by the teachers' lounge, Diego sat at a table of unscored. There was a clear line of sight between him and Imani, and Imani repeatedly stole glances at him, but he never looked over.

Amber and Connor's debate devolved into a verbal slugfest

over the hazards of dating in general, a subject much written about and on which Imani had already made up her mind.

Though it was possible, in theory, to date someone in your own score gang without committing fitness violations, such successes were rare. Dating threatened all of the five elements of fitness: peer group, because there was always the risk that one of you would ascend or descend; impulse control, because you had to keep your hands off each other at least *some* of the time; congruity, because physical desire often conflicted with one's morals; diligence, because it was easy to be distracted by sexual longing at the expense of other priorities, like homework; and rapport, because when you were in the throes of affection, it was common to neglect your other gang members entirely.

Despite all of these hazards, Imani had dated exactly one time. It was sophomore year, and she and her fellow 90 Malachi Beene had been gang buddies for six months. He began flirting with her at lunch, and they commenced what they both agreed would be a score-positive relationship that would avoid all of the well-known hazards.

Then one Friday night at a dance, they'd ended up in a blind spot in the gym behind some risers. The space was already filled with lowbies making out, and Imani had *meant* to resist. But Malachi, taking her silence for acquiescence, plastered his mouth over hers while putting one hand down the back of her jeans and the other one up her shirt. As she pushed him off, he whispered proclamations of physical need so explicit they seemed, to Imani, almost medical. But when he realized she was beyond persuasion, not to mention strong enough to fend him off, he apologized in such a heartfelt way—even *thanking* her for neutralizing his most unfit tendencies—that she'd forgiven him immediately.

Four days later, their new scores were posted.

LeMonde, Imani: 93

Beene, Malachi: 71

The space behind the bleachers hadn't been a blind spot after all. The school had recently convinced Score Corp to spring for an additional eyeball, which hung between two basketball championship banners.

Imani made three decisions that Tuesday: (1) it was over between her and Malachi; (2) that would be her last dance; and (3) she would never date again.

Amber and Connor's debate went nowhere, and, after a while, they resorted to mere repetition of the same themes. When both of them paused for a breather, Deon, fulfilling his quota of unsettling non sequiturs for the day, said: "And what is faith, love, virtue unassayed?"

The gang fell into a stunned silence. Then Amber tented her hands over her nose and said: "Oh my God, you are such a freak." The eyeball wouldn't detect her words, but that didn't mean she'd get away with it.

"Deon," Imani said, "is that a quote from something? Like a book, maybe?"

"Yup," he said.

Amber and Connor resumed their debate, and Deon returned to his sandwich, feeling no need to tell Imani which book the quote was from.

When study period finally arrived, Imani lingered at her locker. The first bell rang, clearing the hallway of most of its students. Note in hand, she glanced up at the nearest eyeball and started to sweat. The late bell rang, and she was alone at last. Imani took a deep breath and prepared to begin her confession. Then, out of the corner of her eye, she saw Mr. Carol through the open door of his classroom. It was a free period for him, and he sat with his feet up on his desk, reading his banged-up tablet while eating potato chips. She shoved the note back in her pocket, wandered over to his doorway, and stood there until he noticed her.

"Imani," he said. "Aren't you going to be late for class?"

"I have study period."

He extended his bag of chips toward her.

"No thanks," she said.

"Did you want to speak to me?" he asked. "Did I forget something in class?"

Mr. Carol routinely forgot things in class, specifically the subject matter he was supposed to be teaching.

"No," Imani said. "I just . . ."

He waved her in while taking his feet off his desk. "Have a seat. You're making me nervous."

Imani glanced back at the eyeball, thought about returning to it, then decided to join Mr. Carol instead. She sat on one of the desks in the circle and let her legs dangle off the edge.

"You seemed preoccupied in class today," he said. "Anything wrong?"

"Nope," she said.

Behind Mr. Carol an eyeball dangled, inches from the top of the American flag.

"Good," he said. "Because I rely on you and Diego in that class, so don't flake out on me. It's depressing enough being a teacher in this day and age. Having a few students with brain cells left is the only thing that keeps me going. Are you sure there's nothing wrong? You look pale."

"Do I?" Her hand went to her cheek.

He nodded. "It's not this final paper, is it? Clarissa's brought in a note from her parents. I'm not caving, by the way. I've done my research. It is in no way score negative."

"Yeah, I know," Imani said. "Can I ask you a question, though?"

"Always."

"Well, I was just wondering. You know when you said we should feel free to collaborate on it?"

Mr. Carol nodded while popping a potato chip in his mouth.

"Did you mean that the scored should collaborate with the unscored?" she asked.

Mr. Carol swallowed. "Would you *like* to collaborate with an unscored?"

Imani shook her head. "I just didn't know what you meant, that's all. I want to make sure I do what you want."

"I see. Imani, are you asking me to *assign* you to collaborate with an unscored?"

The eyeball was directly behind his head, so there was no way it could read his lips, something Imani was certain he knew. She could answer yes or no to his question without implicating herself in any way.

Mr. Carol put his bag of chips down, wiped his hands on his pants, and leaned forward. "Believe you me," he said, "I would like nothing better than to order you to cross the scored-unscored divide to write these papers, but I'm pretty sure that would get me fired. There are places you can go. You know that, right?"

"What do you mean?"

"The library, for one," he said. "Not the school library but the one on the Causeway. God bless your local librarians for keeping at least that public space free of spies. And there are other places too. Certain cafés, bars. Safe zones. I'm just putting it out there. You know, in case you *did* want to collaborate with an unscored, which, of course, I'm not assigning, but . . . well . . . you know what I'm saying."

"Right." Imani knew exactly what he was saying. "Okay. Thanks."

"You're welcome. Hey, and don't be so quiet in class tomorrow."

"Tomorrow's Saturday."

"Shoot. Did I assign reading over the weekend?"

Imani shook her head.

"I really do have to get my act together, don't I?" Mr. Carol picked up the bag of chips and offered her one again.

"No thanks," she said.

When Imani left him, there were still forty minutes of study period remaining, plenty of time to make her confession. But as she paced the empty hallways beneath eyeball after eyeball, with the note in her pocket and her confession ready for airing, she couldn't help but wonder if there was another way of looking at things.

6. homework

THAT NIGHT, IMANI told her parents she was going to the library to meet up with her new gang. It was only a five-minute bike ride, and as she rode beneath the eyeballs, she concluded that there was nothing incriminating about the journey.

The library itself was a different matter. Imani knew that the absence of eyeballs and the presence of unmonitored tablets were an open invitation to every lowbie who wanted to get away with something. They'd go there to download porn or make out in the stacks. It was a den of secret iniquity that even had its own code: "What happens at the library stays at the library." Whether this code was actually followed, however, was doubtful. Most likely, the kids not committing flagrant fitness violations themselves could be found later reporting unfit activities to the nearest eyeball in the hope of improving their own scores. Lowbies were notoriously treacherous.

Imani stood outside the entrance, her bike chained to the rack. There were no other bikes, just one scooter, and in the staff parking area, one small car. Imani had Diego's note in her pocket, and there was an eyeball across the street–the one that would see her enter the library. *If* she entered. It wasn't too late to change her mind. She could cross the street and make her confession right there.

Or she could hear Diego out.

Imani pushed the library doors open. Inside, it was shock-ingly quiet. Behind the curved main desk, a librarian stacked books, her silver hair pulled into a low ponytail. The rest of the empty room yawned in hollow, suffocated silence.

"Can I help you with something?" the librarian asked.

"Just here to browse," Imani lied.

It was hotter than it should have been. The back of Imani's neck dampened beneath the weight of her braid. She unzipped her coat and walked into the low-ceilinged room. Books and papers littered the tables, but there was not a soul in sight. Above a water fountain, an ancient clock ticked clunkily.

In the back, by the fire exit, a black leather jacket was slung over a chair, the only sign of other people. Imani moved toward it, carefully scanning for witnesses. The stacks to her right *appeared* empty, though she couldn't be sure. There was a dance that night, so most likely everyone who would have been committing fitness violations at the library was committing them in the remaining blind spots around the school gym. Diego must have known the library would be empty.

When Imani got to the table where the black jacket hung, she saw Diego a few feet away, leaning against the doorjamb of the fire exit. The door itself was propped open by a trash can, allowing fresh air in. Diego rested one foot on the opposite doorjamb while reading a small, yellowed paperback edition of *1984*.

Without taking his eyes off the book, he said: "You must really want it." He wore a loose white button-down shirt with the sleeves rolled up past his elbows. His bangs were pushed behind his ears, revealing, for the first time, his right eye.

"The scholarship, I mean." He shook his hair free so that it fell back over half his face. Only then did he look at Imani. "You skipped the dance to be here."

"I don't go to dances."

"Me neither. The music sucks." He folded the page down in his book.

"You're not supposed to do that," Imani said. "I think they have bookmarks at the front desk."

"It's my own copy," he said. Then he stared at her with that one visible eye. "So."

"So?" she asked.

"Should we go to the stacks?"

"Absolutely not."

He laughed. "I meant for *privacy*."

Imani looked around. As far as she could see it was just the two of them, plus one old librarian, who didn't know her.

Imani took off her coat and put it on the edge of the table. "Here's fine." She pulled out a chair and sat down, ensuring a sight line to the entrance.

As he walked past, Diego nearly brushed against her, then grabbed his black bag from a chair and dragged it across the table to the other end. He pulled out a curved state-of-the-art smart scroll, a massively expensive hookup.

"Nice tech," Imani said.

"Stolen," he said, then noting her expression added: "Kidding."

"Funny."

"All this tech is just a way station," he said. "Before long, we'll all have a chip in the brain. Actually, we won't even need a brain. Score Corp will do our thinking for us."

"Is that your thesis?"

He laughed, but to Imani it sounded joyless.

"Can I ask you something?" he said.

Imani nodded.

"Why is this okay for you? How are you justifying it?"

"It was your idea."

"Yeah, but I've got nothing to lose. I can hang out with the scored anytime I want. Not that I'd want to."

"Don't worry. We don't want to hang out with you either."

"So why are you here?"

"Because I want that scholarship," she said. "Why do you think?"

"Well, you do have a reputation for self-destruction."

"I have a reputation?"

"It's a gossipy town," he said.

"What are you, from the dark ages or something?" Imani said. "I don't have a reputation. I have a score."

"Hold on." He snapped his scroll open, then raced his long fingers across it. "'I don't have a reputation. I have a score.' Can I quote you?"

Imani pushed her chair back and stood up.

"Wait," he said. "Before you storm out of here in protest, take this."

Imani remained standing, one hand on her coat and both eyes on the door, while he pulled a sheet of paper from his bag and slid it toward her. It was neatly designed, like something you'd find in a textbook.

1) **What advantages do you feel your scored status affords you?**

2) **In what ways is it easier to be scored?**

3) **In what ways is it harder to be scored?**

4) **How is society improved by the score?**

Between each question, there were lined spaces for the answers.

"Wait a minute," Imani said. "Did *you* write this?"

"Yeah." Diego stood and slid into his leather jacket, revealing the faint traces of sweat marks under his arms. "Leave it on your desk in American history," he said. "I'll pick it up after class. And don't worry, I'll be sneaky."

"*You're* giving *me* homework?"

"If I like what you've written, I'll be in touch."

Diego headed to the front door, nodding to the silver-haired librarian, who said his name as if they were old pals. A few moments later, a generic factory hum from a scooter started up, then faded northward, carving the route of his journey home.

Imani was still standing at the end of the table, holding his homework assignment.

"What an assho—"

Imani never swore. It was a severe violation of impulse control. But she almost finished that sentence.

Out loud.

7. big ideas

IMANI WOULD HAVE liked to spend the following Saturday in Cady's garage, handing over tools while discussing Diego's risky proposal. It wasn't that Cady's advice would have been trustworthy. Her ideas were formed in the steamy jungle of emotion rather than the cool laboratory of reason. But she would have listened. Cady was a world-class listener, attentive even while soldering a circuit board.

Imani knew that her parents would not have understood. Their grasp of the world was based on an obsolete value system that was probably the root of Imani's problems. Who else had gifted her with the dusty antique of loyalty, that "disempowering bond"?

Isiah might have understood, but his advice would be worthless. Imani knew she was beyond the machinations of middle school fitness. She was at best in the realm of extreme subtlety. At worst, she was beginning a downward spiral that would deliver her, with mathematical finality, into her destiny of worms.

Or worse.

So with her options limited, Imani went clamming. The shores of Hogg Island were desolate early Saturday morning as she waited for the tide to recede. Frankenwhaler was beached at her side, the sun rising warm and bright over the plateau of Corona Point. She had only herself to speak to, and did so freely.

There was much to consider. The risks of a secret collaboration with Diego were obvious. Not only was there the threat of discovery, there was also the prospect of carrying around the damning secret in full view of every eyeball in Somerton. Knowingly committing an unfit act was the essence of incongruity. What if the software inferred this violation of the third element from a persistently guilty expression? Could she fool it? Or would the attempt result in her score dropping even further? What nonmilitary options were there for a 52? Or a 42?

On the other hand, the benefits of collaborating with Diego were obvious too. He was smart, as much as Imani hated to admit it, very smart. His anti-score sentiments were original and well sourced. Though she found his attitude grating, there was a good reason he was Mr. Carol's favorite. Not that Imani derided her own gifts. She knew she wrote excellent essays, with a sharp grasp of point and counterpoint. She had excellent critical reasoning skills, as Mr. Carol himself had frequently told her. But she also knew what she lacked: a passion for the big ideas. She could turn almost anything into an exemplary essay, but to win the Otis Scholarship, she'd need more than that. She'd need a sense of purpose. She'd need the kind of passionate opposition to the score that Diego displayed so skillfully.

As the tide receded, the damp sand began to bubble. Imani got to work, filling her mesh bag with the oversized clams her mother would turn into a thick, creamy chowder. If she'd been born twenty years earlier, perhaps Imani would have settled into a life working those shores, as her mother's family had done for generations, before most of the commercial clam operations closed down. She paused to gaze across the channel. Sometimes she found it hard to believe that such rich surroundings could be so bereft of life, that beneath her beloved blue was a tragedy still unfolding. How had people let it happen? If Imani had a sense of purpose for anything, it was for this: the river, the islands, the ocean beyond, and the interplay of commerce and nature that she knew from her parents' musings had once been Somerton's backbone–before it was a trial town, before it *needed* to be a trial town. There was a time when Somerton had taken care of itself.

Imani's clam fork stuck out of the sand where she squatted. Her bag was full, the sun was high, and there was just enough water in the river to carry her home.

Mrs. LeMonde was on her knees in the kitchen, making room on the bottom shelf of the refrigerator for a new box of night crawlers. Her faded black cargo pants had frayed irreparably at the ankles. Her mother only bought new clothes when the old ones disintegrated.

Imani lifted her clam bag into the sink, and her mother stood to inspect the haul. Mrs. LeMonde loved nothing more than to spend all day in the kitchen with a sink full of fresh catch.

"Anyone else out there?" she asked.

"Nope."

Stuffing her hair behind her ears, Mrs. LeMonde turned on the faucet and got to work. She looked beautiful to Imani, her auburn hair messy with waves and shot through with silver, her freckled skin crinkling around the eyes. She belonged there, in the house and at the marina, in the bait shop and in her own destiny of worms. But Imani knew that her mother's way of life could disintegrate, like those cargo pants, at any minute. A few more recreational boaters opting for Waverly, another lobsterman calling it a day, and the marina was done for. The problem with Somerton was that it produced great fishermen, clammers, lobstermen, and boat mechanics. But no one had tended to the foundation. No one was taking care of the river itself.

"Something on your mind?" her mother asked.

"Nope."

Her mother laughed. "Of course not. You know, I had secrets once too."

Imani would have liked to hear those secrets someday, but not now. She had work to do. She was going to college in the fall. No matter what it took.

* * *

Though it galled Imani that Diego believed she had to prove her worth to him, she was willing to play along. This would not entail any attempt to be his friend, however. She would use his ideas, as he would use hers. There would be no more to it than that. She settled down on her bed and got to work.

The first three questions were easy. After a few drafts, she came up with the following answers:

1) What advantages do you feel your scored status affords you?

Answer: In addition to the obvious advantages, such as access to a college education and to the better jobs, there's the opportunity to achieve the contentedness of constant self-improvement. Whereas the unscored must accept what they are and muddle through life permanently flawed, the scored receive monthly feedback from an impartial and highly intelligent source, which empowers us to change.

2) In what ways is it easier to be scored?

Answer: In no way. In fact, it's much harder to be scored.

3) In what ways is it harder to be scored?

Answer: In every way. We are under constant pressure to maintain or improve our scores. It is much easier to drop than it is to rise. Our peer groups change suddenly, and we are punished for attempting

friendship outside of gang boundaries. We are forced
to walk the line between observable fitness and
punishable gamesmanship. And we can never relax
until the last score is in.

So far so good, Imani thought. But when she got to question 4—*How is society improved by the score?*—she spent a lot of time staring through her window. To identify how the score had improved society, you had to consider what society would be like without it. But she had never lived in that society. From her parents' stories, she knew that it had been no picnic, that a prolonged depression had wrung out the nation and made places like Somerton almost unlivable. She knew about the high unemployment rate, and the concentration of wealth that still made her father spit fire about "the man." It wasn't as if the score had fixed all of those things—yet. Wealth was still highly concentrated, as the millionaire crust of Corona Point attested, but the score *was* spreading. It was becoming "ubiquitous," to borrow a favorite term of the creepers. And it wasn't free anymore. Somerton, Wakachee, and the handful of other trial towns had been test cases for Score Corp. In other towns, Imani knew, you had to pay for the privilege of being scored.

And people did pay, by the *millions*. That had to mean something.

Imani recalled an assignment Mr. Carol had given them earlier in the year. He frequently asked them to examine current events in order to highlight historical principles, and this time he'd assigned the Somerton pages of WickedNews, an online clearinghouse of local news for the North Shore area. There, on the Education Forum, the parents of Somerton had been waging a debate about barring all unscored students from the school system. Mr. Carol had asked his students to uncover constitutional principles at stake, but Imani had found few.

She called up WickedNews on her cell and scanned through the debate again. The letters were full of venom, bad grammar, and personal attacks. The unscored parents, or "opt-outs," as they preferred to be called, were vastly outnumbered, fielding only four dogs in the fight, whereas the scored letters were often signed by twenty or more parents. Though the letter writers displayed that selfishness common to parents (a selfishness that extends exactly one degree outward, to incorporate one's own children but no one else's), they also frequently insisted that whatever was in their child's interest was in society's interest too. For the most part, this amounted to the parents of the unscored fearing a surveillance state and mind control, while the parents of the scored insisted they were heralding a new age of mental health and meritocracy. There were links aplenty in support of each position.

Though Imani had never been interested in politics, it occurred to her now, as she pinged from one link to another in the no-holds-barred brawl of parental panic, that she'd been living in a bit of a bubble. Outside the confines of her own small concerns, a war of ideas was under way. After wading into those churning waters for a few hours, she was able to piece together the following answer to question 4:

Since the introduction of the score, there has been a measurable decline in the following antisocial behaviors among children and teens: burglary and theft, drug use, unplanned pregnancy, truancy, vandalism, and drop-out rates. For the fittest teens, the score opens a pathway to higher education by providing a full scholarship to any state school. This benefits not only the recipients but also society as a whole, by enlarging the pool of candidates from which tomorrow's leaders will come. Employers report benefiting from the score as a result of having an objective means of evaluating an applicant's character, whereas in the past they could only make subjective judgments. Without the score, we would be living in an unstable aristocracy.

Imani attached links from the *American Journal of Psychology, Business Today,* and Mr. Carol's personal favorite, the *New York Times.* There was no shortage of counterevidence, and it intrigued her that, based on her research, she could have come up with a very different answer. But that wasn't the deal. Besides, she knew Diego would have the counterevidence already in hand.

Imani turned the paper over and wrote as neatly as possible:

I've answered your questions to the best of my abilities, but, if you don't mind my saying so, I found your line of inquiry obvious and not likely to lead to a compelling thesis.

To justify my risk in working with you, could YOU please answer the following questions?

1) Do you oppose all technological progress or just some? Be specific.
2) In the absence of the score, how would you address teen crime, delinquency, drug use, pregnancy, and other antisocial behaviors?
3) Do you believe the human psyche is knowable and changeable?
4) Explain your hair. Seriously. What's up with that?

Diego wasn't the only one who could assign homework.

8. together

AT FIRST, IMANI was too self-conscious about the note she was carrying to worry about all the whispering; in the halls of Somerton High, people were always whispering. The note was folded in quarters and jammed into the change pocket of her jeans, where, despite the implausibility, she could not resist wondering if the eyeballs would detect it. She felt clammy and wasn't sure whether nervousness would make her redden or go pale. Neither option was acceptable. If she was going to undertake this secret collaboration with Diego Landis, she'd have to work on managing her emotions.

The whispering grew more feverish as Imani neared her locker, and finally she noticed that much of it was directed at her. Eyes darted toward her, then away, then upward to the eyeballs.

She was being discussed.

There was only one explanation she could think of. The librarian must have ratted her out. She was someone's grandmother, perhaps, and had mentioned it, maybe even innocently, over dinner. Imani could see the whole scene. Peas being passed while the librarian described an argument between Diego Landis, that unscored kid with the strange hair, and some mixed-race girl with caramel skin (Imani's skin was always described by white people as caramel or cappuccino) and the most *adorable* freckles. That would be it. That would be the detail that would give her away. The librarian's grandchild—a lowbie, no doubt—would tell his gang buddies, and, through the magic of exponential rumor dissemination, Imani's secret collaboration with Diego would be a matter of public record within hours. Her score was ruined.

Then she saw Cady and Parker.

They stood at Cady's locker, holding hands. The sight of them together, so brazen and unapologetic, stopped Imani short.

That was what all the whispering was about. And the eyes darting toward and away from Imani were not condemning eyes, they were anticipatory. Everyone was waiting to see how Imani would react to Cady's return, and to this open flouting of the divide between scored and unscored.

As the late bell rang, Cady and Parker walked hand in hand across the hall to Cady's homeroom. Parker leaned down, kissed Cady on the forehead, and walked away.

Without even trying, Imani gave the eyeballs, and her

fellow students, a flawless performance. She was as shocked as anyone at the audacity of her friend's behavior. Not only were Cady and Parker not hiding their relationship, they seemed to be making a stand.

By the end of first period, Imani had heard several versions of the same story: Cady and Parker had shown up at the gym for the dance on Friday night. They had danced with each other for three songs—one of them a slow song. There'd been no unfit behavior on the dance floor, the rumor mill was willing to concede, but Cady and Parker were definitely "together," a state of affairs variously described as "full on," "in your face," and "balls to the wall" (the last one being the contribution of lowbies). They had made no attempt to speak to anyone, and no one spoke to them. Finally, they'd snuck out the back to make out (it was presumed) or to have sex by the Dumpsters. At some point, they'd taken a can of spray paint and written "Free the unscored" on the brick wall outside the gym. There were no witnesses, just one eyeball with a sight line to the wall. Only the software would know if they were truly guilty. And only Cady would pay if they were.

In American history, Imani threw herself into Mr. Carol's discussion of civil liberties, taking down both Logan and Rachel with well-sourced arguments, courtesy of the weekend's descent into the link-riddled debate on WickedNews. She even engaged Diego a few times, agreeing once and disagreeing twice, without ever looking at him. When the bell rang, Imani left the note on her desk, then headed to the door, without looking back. Once out in the hall, Diego brushed past her, his knuckles grazing her forearm. She could see the edge of the note in his hand as he tucked it carefully but nonchalantly in the back pocket of his jeans.

It was an audacious game they were playing. Imani knew the software was designed—or more accurately, had *evolved*—to peel away the hidden layers of the teenage mind. But it seemed too late to turn back now. The damage was done and her clock was ticking.

9. the f word

THE NEXT MORNING, Imani found the note in her locker, sitting on top of her calculus book. Diego must have slipped it through the vent. She slid it carefully into her front pocket, then rushed to the girls' room.

Being eyeball-free, the girls' room was crammed with lowbies who went there to share secrets, spread rumors, and express foulmouthed outrage at being the subjects of secrets and rumors. Imani had never understood lowbies. For all their noise and backstabbing, few of them rose significantly. They'd slug it out over the line between 29 and 30, a doom zone she'd never contemplated. That was Cady's zone now. Employment opportunities: nil. A lot of those girls would enlist. Some of them would get pregnant in order to qualify for welfare—and avoid having to enlist.

Imani averted her eyes, locked herself into a stall, and unfolded Diego's note. Above her own questions, Diego had written the following in his tiny handwriting:

I have serious issues with your answers, which I'd like to discuss in person at some point. Until then, here are my answers to your questions:

1) Do you oppose all technological progress or just some? Be specific.

Answer: This question is beneath even you. Of course I don't oppose all technological progress. I'll keep the bicycle and the Internet, thanks. Also antibiotics, rocket technology, and the electric bass. You can keep Score Corp, WMD, and the automobile. Is that specific enough, or do you require a comprehensive list?

Clearly, she'd hit a nerve.

2) In the absence of the score, how would you address teen crime, delinquency, drug use, pregnancy, and other antisocial behaviors?

Answer: I wouldn't. Those things have always existed, and why shouldn't they? In a society as broken as ours, "antisocial" behavior is the only behavior worth defending.

Imani laughed. Was Diego honestly endorsing teen pregnancy?

3) Do you believe the human psyche is knowable and changeable?

Answer: I believe the human psyche is only partially knowable. Any attempt to reduce it to a finite problem is doomed to failure. As for changeability, sure, people change all the time. But Score Corp isn't just trying to change people, it's trying to reengineer them into things it can control.

Paranoid, Imani thought. And vague.

4) Explain your hair. Seriously. What's up with that?

Answer: Fuck you.

Imani gasped. The word was even more potent in written form, the *F* so aggressive in its rightward lean.

Below this, in handwriting so small it was hard to imagine it came from a human hand, Diego had written:

Incidentally, you passed my test (barely). So if you want to keep going, let's meet someplace where we can actually talk. How about Rita Mae's tonight at 7? There's an eyeball-free route to it via the back alley behind the ice rink on Lake Road. Just exit through the back door by the vending machines.

DL, the "permanently flawed" one

That night, while washing the dishes with Isiah, Imani told her parents she was going to the library again to meet up with her gang. Her parents applauded her efforts toward her new "friends," though her dad still thought it was a "damn shame" about Cady and looked forward to seeing her hanging around the marina again.

"I hear she's a vandal now," Isiah said.

They'd finished the dishes, and Isiah was standing with his back to the counter, arms folded across his chest, an errant soap bubble floating behind his head.

Imani popped the bubble with her finger. "There were no witnesses," she said.

"There was an eyeball."

"Doesn't matter. You can't request the footage." She hung her damp dish towel neatly over a drawer handle.

"Why not?" he asked.

Imani shook her head at his ignorance. "Proprietary information," she said. "Score Corp *never* turns over footage."

"What if there's a murder?"

"Doesn't matter," she said. "They own it."

"So if there's a murder, and it's caught on camera, the cops can't get, like, a court order or something?"

"Well, this isn't exactly murder, Isiah. It's graffiti. And anyway, I doubt it was her."

"Why?"

"It's not her style."

"Why are you defending her?"

Their father sat at the kitchen table sorting through the crumpled receipts he kept littered on the floor of his truck. "Everyone has a right to a defense, Isiah," he said. "That's the law."

Mrs. LeMonde came in, tapped her husband on the shoulder, and held a receipt in front of him.

"Drill bit?" he guessed.

Mrs. LeMonde sighed. She was the bookkeeper in the family. "Imani, don't be out too late," she said. Then she returned to the living room.

"Your mother's a genius with those numbers," her father said.

She had to be, Imani thought. There were fewer boats moored at the marina every year. But the bills only grew.

The hockey rink was only ten minutes away by bicycle. Imani considered taking her skates for cover, but she didn't want to raise suspicions with her parents. Besides, she figured if the software was smart enough to form an opinion about her presence at the rink, it was smart enough to know there was no free skate on Tuesday nights. Most likely, the footage of her riding to the ice rink would be discarded as insignificant. At least, that was what she hoped.

Inside, the rink itself had limited coverage—about half of the ice and some of the stands. Ice bullies knew that if they wanted to inflict pain out of coverage, they had to do it on the side of the rink closest to the skate rental window.

On the ice was an over-the-hill league, clashing and tangling to the *chirp chirp* of the referee's whistle. Nobody watched in the stands. She walked quickly to the back, past the skate rental window, where the owner sharpened a blade with a ferocious screech. In the back, behind the parked Zamboni, was a stuffy room crammed with vending machines, including one ancient behemoth that dispensed watery cocoa into paper cups. When Imani was young, she would beg her parents for money after skating lessons just so she could watch that little cup drop down to receive the stream of cocoa. It seemed like magic. When she thought of it now, it seemed impossible that her parents had ever been able to afford skating lessons for both her and Isiah. Her dad must have bartered something big.

Nowadays, to keep Isiah in hockey, he let the assistant coach trailer his boat for free.

Outside, the wind was still, and the only sound was the buzz of some machine jutting from the back of the building. The cobbled alley, once a bridle path, curved into the distance, making it impossible to see all the way to the end. There were no eyeballs in view, so Imani set out for Rita Mae's.

The alley was bordered by woods on one side and, on the other, by derelict warehouses rumored to house no end of vagrants, rapists, deviants, and ghosts, depending on whom you asked. Imani didn't believe those stories, but the place did have a haunted feel. Around a bend in the path, something dangled from a rotting telephone pole. But only when she was directly underneath it could she identify what it was: the remains of an eyeball, its innards torn free but still attached. Score Corp normally replaced damaged eyeballs, but this one looked as if it had been hanging there for months.

Imani kept walking. The derelict warehouses were behind her now, leaving only woods on either side. Eventually, two male voices drifted toward her, their laughter battered by the wind shifting through the trees. When they came into view, Imani pegged them immediately as private school guys, possibly Corona Pointers. They wore expensive clothes, but sloppily, and had expensive longish haircuts, also worn sloppily. Imani put her head down to avoid eye contact, but a pause in their chatter indicated they'd noticed her.

"Hey, clamdiggah," one of them said, in the exaggerated

accent of the working class. Imani didn't cross paths with rich kids often, but she knew enough not to be surprised by the remark. Imani didn't mind the label, but she wondered what it was about her appearance that gave her away.

"Hey, are you black or white?" one of them asked. He was a white boy himself, tall and narrow with thin lips and cold eyes. His friend, also white, was short with red hair and freckles. They both stumbled slightly as they approached. They were drunk, and the kind of people her father loved to hate.

"You scored?" the tall one asked. "'Cause we're unscored, but shhh, we won't tell anyone if you don't."

Imani wanted to run, but she didn't want them to know she was afraid.

"So what are you?" The freckled one stopped and waited for her. "Lowbie or highbie?"

"Definitely a lowbie." The tall one stopped too.

"No, she looks uptight," the freckled one replied.

"What's she doing here, then? Hey, are you black or white? Not that it matters or anything. I'm just curious."

They both stood waiting, expecting her to stop and chat with them.

Imani walked by, noting the way their heads followed her.

"Clamdiggah," the tall one said. "I give her two chances." He raised his voice to ensure she heard him. "One, she's swinging around a pole in a few years. Two, land mine food."

The freckled one laughed with a tinge of embarrassment. "Man, that's cold."

"She does have a sexy walk, though," the tall one went on. "Hey, you know you have a sexy walk? And I'm okay with the race thing. Seriously. No? Still not interested? What about now?".

Imani could feel their eyes on her as she willed herself to walk, not run, away from them. As the sound of their chuckling faded, a single thought cheered her: one day the score would be universal. There would be eyeballs everywhere, even in that haunted pathway. You'd need a score to go to college, a score to get a job. Maybe you'd even need a score to go to high school. Privilege would be wiped out, and boys like that would get what they deserved.

The path took Imani to Chester Road. Across the street, the sign for Rita Mae's hung from a gnarled wooden pole, its swirly lettering draping a chipped red rose. It was the only building on the road—a shingled shack, barely larger than the ice-fishing houses people dragged onto the nearby lake. A warm glow emanated from within, along with the sweet pungent smell of a wood fire.

Imani approached slowly, scanning the trees for eyeballs and finding none. Next to the entrance was a window, framed by heavy gold curtains. She peered through it, reluctant to enter. She could see Diego in the back by a wood-burning stove, reading a small paperback. None of his friends were there, just a handful of teenagers she didn't recognize and some adults eating dinner or sipping pints of beer. They weren't the kind of people her parents knew. They weren't members of the bowling league or "retired" clammers. The teenagers looked more like those boys in the alley than like anyone she knew.

Though Mr. Carol hadn't mentioned Rita Mae's by name, she knew that it was one of those places he'd described: a so-called safe zone, beyond the score's reach. But safe was the last thing Imani felt. The encounter in the alley had depleted her courage. She doubted she could stride in there now, take a seat next to Diego Landis, and pretend she belonged there. She didn't belong. She was a "clamdiggah." And these people were not.

Diego saw her through the window. He put his book on the table and waited for her to join him. Imani resented his calm, resented him for the disequilibrium of their states. All she could think was *run*.

So that was what she did, pausing only to look back when she heard the door to Rita Mae's open and shut.

"Imani!" Diego shouted. He hadn't put his coat on. "Where are you going?"

She kept running. Halfway to the ice rink, near the vandalized eyeball, she heard footsteps behind her. She sped up, but Diego was fast, arriving at the ice rink moments before her and blocking her way.

"What the fuck?" he said. The wind jostled his hair, revealing the surprising symmetry of his face.

"Can you please move?" Imani said, out of breath.

Diego hugged his thin black sweater against the cold. "Why did you run away?"

"I changed my mind."

"Why?"

"Can you please move?"

"No," he said. "Not until you tell me why you changed your mind."

But Imani wasn't sure why she'd changed her mind. It hadn't been a rational choice. It had been something closer to physical. "It's not safe there," she said.

"It's completely safe. It's Rita Mae's."

"So?"

"So my parents know her personally," he said. "If any one of her customers ever ratted out a scored kid for being there, she'd kill them. Like, with her bare hands. It's kind of the code there. Rita Mae's is a safe zone. Trust me."

"There are no safe zones," Imani said. "That's a lowbie concept."

"Is it?"

"Yes," she said. "And one that constantly undermines them."

"Why?"

"You really don't get it," she said.

"Yeah, well, that's why you're here, right?" he said. "To teach me. And incidentally, there are plenty of things you don't get either."

"Well, let's leave it that way."

Imani reached around him for the door handle, but he grabbed her wrist. She yanked her arm free and he let go instantly, but remained pressed against the door.

"What are you afraid of?" he asked.

She stared back at him, feeling hot despite the cold. She

wanted to tell him she feared nothing, and certainly not him. But the truth was she feared *everything*. She feared being caught in that alley. She feared hiding things from the eyeballs. She feared taking this risk to collaborate with him and she feared *not* taking the risk. She feared the way Diego reminded her of those boys in the alley.

"Nothing," she said. "I just changed my mind."

He stood his ground for a few seconds, then stepped away from the door. "Fine," he said. "But you'll never win that scholarship."

"Neither will you," she said. Then she opened the door and left him in the cold.

10. spies

AT THE END of school the next day, Imani caught a glimpse of Ms. Wheeler through the glass wall of the reception area. She was crisp and stylish in her pale pink suit as she explained something apparently complicated to Mrs. Bronson. Imani had not yet forgiven Ms. Wheeler for dashing her hopes during their last meeting. But as she watched her bent over a tablet with Mrs. Bronson, discussing, perhaps, the fate of another student, Imani wondered if it was precisely that directness that she most needed right now. After all, you didn't get ahead by *avoiding* the hard choices. She decided to exploit Ms. Wheeler's open-door policy one more time.

"I don't understand," Ms. Wheeler said when Imani followed her into her office. Ms. Wheeler signaled for Mrs. Bronson to leave them alone with a wave of the hand, which Mrs. Bronson did, reluctantly. Ms. Wheeler closed her office door, then looked at the note, which Imani had handed her. "He wants you to help him write this . . . this . . ." She looked at Imani, perplexed. "What is it exactly?"

"It's for our final essay in American history," Imani explained. "Mr. Carol's going to submit them to the Otis Institute for a scholarship."

"The Otis Institute? I've never heard of it." Ms. Wheeler sat down, unfurled her tap pad, and began typing, the information flickering in her specs. "Oh, I see. It's one of these educational advocacy groups. Tom Carol should not be withholding this information. This scholarship should be open to everyone."

"It is," Imani said. "But I guess not many people know about it."

"And the subject he's assigned is *opposing the score*?"

"Only for the scored," Imani said. "The unscored have to *defend* the score."

"You're kidding"

"Mr. Carol thought it would make our essays stand out," Imani explained.

"Uh-huh." Ms. Wheeler continued typing for a few seconds, then blinked away the flickering lights from her specs and turned her full gaze on Imani. "Do you want to know the most dangerous word in education?"

"What?"

" 'Tenure.' " Ms. Wheeler picked up the note and squinted at it. "Such small handwriting."

"So the eyeballs couldn't read it."

"Of course." Ms. Wheeler nodded. "So. Diego Landis. He's an excellent student. I'll give him that. Especially for an unscored."

"Yeah, I know," Imani said.

"Enrolled here his junior year, and was promptly suspended for defacing an eyeball and getting into a shoving match with Brian Pilsner."

"I remember that," Imani said.

"Claimed he was set up," Ms. Wheeler said. "He's got quite a disciplinary record, actually." She resumed typing. "Disrupting class, some graffiti." She brightened at the word. "I'd forgotten about that."

Ms. Wheeler had offered one hundred dollars to anyone with information about the graffiti artists responsible for "Free the unscored," but so far no one had been officially accused.

"I've had my eye on him," Ms. Wheeler continued. "He's been quiet lately. Hasn't caused any trouble since"–her fingers tapped–"February." She blinked away her specs' display and looked at Imani with a furrowed brow. "Did you want to make an official complaint about him?"

"A complaint?"

"Isn't that why you're here?"

Imani stalled.

"Wait a minute," Ms. Wheeler leaned forward. "You're not here because you want to *accept* Diego's proposal, are you?"

When Imani failed to answer, Ms. Wheeler leaned back in her chair and removed her specs. "Oh, I see," she said. "You want that scholarship, don't you? That Otis thing."

Imani wanted that scholarship more than she'd ever wanted anything. "I think I could win it," she said. "I think I have a shot."

Ms. Wheeler laughed gently. "And I thought you were here to report Diego Landis for harassment."

"Well, he does have a sort of harassing personality," Imani conceded. "But I think he could actually help me. He's pretty smart, especially about anti-score stuff."

"Oh, I don't doubt that." Ms. Wheeler lifted a pile of papers from her desk and produced a tablet. "Do you know *why* he's so smart about anti-score stuff?" She made a few taps, then turned the tablet around to show Imani. On the screen was an article from the *Boston Globe* about a Somerton lawyer engaged in a legal battle with the school system. There was a photo of Ms. Wheeler next to a woman who was identified in the caption as Dena Landis.

"Is that—"

"Diego's mother," Ms. Wheeler said. "She's a lawyer. And a good one too. Do you have any idea how much she and her little band of opt-outs cost this school in legal fees last year?"

Imani shook her head.

"Two hundred and eighty-six *thousand* dollars," Ms. Wheeler said. "Claims of harassment, unequal treatment, unlawful surveillance. The state's making local school districts cover those costs now. Imagine that. We had to lay off staff to pay for it."

"Like that history teacher?"

"And a French teacher and an art teacher. Yes. And don't think it's over. Dena Landis is connected. Every creeper group in the country is in her corner. I know what her strategy is too. The nuisance lawsuit. She's trying to break our bank. She wants to make it fiscally impossible for us to keep fighting her."

"I had no idea."

"Old money," Ms. Wheeler said. "Deep pockets. They live on Corona Point, you know?"

Imani's mouth dropped open. She'd always known there was something unique about Diego, something that separated him from the other unscored at Somerton High. But she'd never figured him for a Corona Pointer.

"These people have no respect for people like you and me," Ms. Wheeler went on. "They have theirs, and they don't want anyone else to have a shot. Sure, she talks a good game about protecting public education for opt-outs like her son, but you know what I think?" Ms. Wheeler leaned over the desk, her eyes flashing. "I think she enrolled her son here just so they'd have grounds to sue."

"Really?"

"I think Diego's a spy, if you want to know the truth."

"A *spy?*"

Ms. Wheeler nodded silently, as if she'd just shared a confidence. Imani felt honored by it. She doubted Ms. Wheeler was so forthcoming with any other students.

Ms. Wheeler sat back in her chair and regarded Imani. "I have to say I think it's very interesting that Diego's turned his attention to you."

"Why?"

"You're a perfect case study now. A fast dropper. That's

probably why he picked you. Maybe you'll end up as the star of Dena Landis's next case against the score."

The thought sickened Imani. "I don't want to be a case study," she said.

"I don't blame you."

"I should spy on *him*," Imani said.

Ms. Wheeler grew serious. "What do you mean by that?"

Imani wasn't sure what she'd meant by it. But now that she'd blurted it out, it took shape as a viable plan. "What if I asked him questions about his mother and her work?"

"Do you think he'd answer you?"

"It was his idea to collaborate in the first place. We're supposed to be teaching each other about our point of view. Look."

Imani took out Diego's "homework" assignment from her bag and handed it to her. Ms. Wheeler took her time reading it.

"Nice language," Ms. Wheeler said. "I like *your* answers, though. 'Without the score, we would be living in an unstable aristocracy.' Very insightful. But I don't understand. It looks to me like you've already accepted his proposal."

"Well, I did, but..."

"But what?"

"But I changed my mind."

Ms. Wheeler slumped slightly in her chair. "I see."

"I thought it was worth the risk," Imani explained. "But the thing is, if I don't win the scholarship and I get caught with Diego—"

"You'll drop like a stone," Ms. Wheeler said.

"Exactly."

There was a pause as Ms. Wheeler stared at the note, swiveling gently in her cream leather chair. "If only there were some score-positive way to accept Diego's proposal," she said. "Some justification that the software would view in a positive light."

"Yeah, but the unscored are off-limits," Imani said. "That's the first element. That's peer group."

"True." Ms. Wheeler resumed swiveling. "But it's not as if you'd be doing it for fun."

"God, no."

"It's not as if you'd be *dating* him."

Imani laughed sharply. The idea of dating Diego Landis was too ridiculous to ponder, especially now that she knew where he came from, and what he was doing at Somerton High. "Wait a minute," Imani said. "Wouldn't it mean something that I was obtaining useful information about a creeper lawyer who's fighting against the score?"

Ms. Wheeler stopped swiveling. "What do you mean?"

"Well, it's like you said. I wouldn't be associating with Diego Landis for fun. I'd be doing it for . . ." Imani looked up at the ceiling as she searched for the right words.

"For the sake of the score?" Ms. Wheeler offered.

"Yeah," Imani said. "Exactly. To protect the score against its enemies. That has to count for something, right?"

Ms. Wheeler bit her lip. "The software *is* smarter than us," she said. "It knows our motives even when we don't."

"And this would be a fit motive," Imani insisted. "Wouldn't it?"

Ms. Wheeler sank back into the thick cushiony leather of her chair and swiveled gently. It was her own nervous habit,

Imani realized, her principal's version of shining her tap screen. "This is uncharted territory, Imani."

"But it could work, right?"

Ms. Wheeler stared right through her, a smile playing at the corners of her mouth. "I wouldn't rule it out," she said.

It was considerably less than the assurance Imani was hoping for, but it was something.

"One problem, though," Ms. Wheeler said. "Won't Diego suspect something if you agree to openly collaborate with him?"

Imani paused to think about this. "I'll sneak around with him. It was his suggestion to be discreet."

"And how will the software interpret that?"

Imani sighed. There were too many tangles in this growing web.

"Of course," Ms. Wheeler said, "you could make a preemptive confession. Tell an eyeball what you're planning to do beforehand. Lay it all on the line so the software knows what you're doing and why you're doing it."

Now it was Imani's turn to bite her lip. The idea of speaking directly to an eyeball continued to frighten her. "I guess I could do that," she said.

"You'd have to be completely honest," Ms. Wheeler warned.

"I could do that," Imani whispered.

"Otherwise it's gaming."

"I wouldn't be gaming," she said.

"Well." Ms. Wheeler leaned forward with a friendly and conspiratorial smile. "You'd be gaming Diego Landis."

"True," Imani said.

"And his mother," Ms. Wheeler added.

But this, Imani thought, was an unexpected bonus.

There were seventeen eyeballs between school and home, but Imani waited until she got to Marina Road. Then she ran across to Abruzzi Antiques, an establishment so unpatronized it was more hobby than business. The OPEN sign hung in the door, but the elderly Mrs. Abruzzi was nowhere to be seen. In the disused parking lot were an ancient phone booth and a menagerie of crumbling seagull-fouled garden sculptures. Standing like a guard at the foot of a street lamp from which hung an eyeball was a cement elephant about four feet high. Dropping her backpack, Imani climbed onto the elephant's back and stood up. This brought her closer to an eyeball than she'd ever been before. Its shiny black surface reflected the sun so perfectly it hurt her eyes.

"Hi," Imani said to it, then paused, enslaved by the conventions of dialogue. "I guess I don't have to introduce myself because you already know who I am, right? I'm Imani LeMonde?" She knew something was tracking her words, something far away in a central processing station, some nonphysical thing made of ones and zeroes. It read her lips and formed a judgment sounder than any she could form. "So I'm here to confess something I'm about to do," she said. "And I want to be completely honest with you. I'm going to be spending time with an unscored named Diego Landis. It's not because I like him or anything. I actually find him..." Imani's gaze drifted upward as she searched for the right words.

"Annoying," she said. "And foulmouthed. So there will be swearing. I mean, *I* won't be swearing, but he will. Anyway, my original reason for doing this was research for a paper. There's a scholarship given by the Otis Institute, which I'm sure you can look up or whatever. And then I learned that Diego is the son of a creeper lawyer who has been suing the school. So I thought that I could use my connection with Diego to learn about his mother's plans to fight . . . well, to fight *you*."

Imani stared at the small black ball, which seemed suddenly fragile.

"They want to destroy you," she said, "because they don't believe in upward mobility and all the things you've promised." She swallowed, knowing the software would process the gesture according to its own superior logic. "But I do," she said.

She wasn't gaming. She *did* believe in the things the score promised. At least, she thought she did. She'd never found any reason *not* to believe in them.

When she climbed down from the stone elephant, she came face to face with an armless mermaid. The pitted thing had been through blizzards, heat waves, and callous movers only to wind up in that parking lot in Somerton. Still, as it gazed beyond the pizza shop toward the ocean, which would always elude it, somehow it managed to look hopeful.

11. clamdigger

THE NEXT DAY, Imani waited until the break before final period, then slipped a note into Diego's locker with an invitation to meet her in person. A junior 80 saw her and would probably rat her out for it. But it wouldn't matter, because Imani had already ratted herself out.

That afternoon, a few hours after high tide, Imani took Frankenwhaler up the river to a small strip of beach belonging to the Wentworths, a couple who went bowling with her parents once a week. Their ramshackle house was obscured by overgrown trees that were rapidly swallowing what was left of their beach. A three-wheeled ATV sat catty-corner to a shredded badminton net, and strewn about like seaweed was an assortment of plastic toys that belonged to their grandchild.

It was cool and overcast, no shadows anywhere, the sky a

uniform gray. Imani pulled on a sweater and waited. It felt strange to be picking up someone other than Cady. She wondered if Cady missed their afternoons on the river or if she preferred spending her time with Parker.

In the distance, she heard a low hum. It was nothing like Frankenscooter's, but Imani could feel her heart beat anyway. As the sound grew, she tidied up the boat, folding the blanket and wiping down the bench. Eventually, a black scooter appeared between two trees, jolted over a big root, then skidded onto the sand. Without stopping, it came across the beach, swerved around two baby dolls, then stopped abruptly next to the ATV.

Diego didn't dismount right away. He took in the surroundings first, hidden behind the visor of his black helmet. "So you have your own boat," he said finally. "Fancy."

Imani stepped out and dragged the boat sideways onto the beach. "Get in."

Diego stowed his helmet in his trunk, then climbed into Imani's boat and sat on the rear bench, right by the motor. Imani looked at him, confused, but he stared back innocently.

"Uh, I think *I'll* drive," Imani said.

"Oh, sorry." Diego shifted to the middle bench.

"Have you ever been on a boat?" Imani asked, making no effort to keep the condescension out of her tone.

"Once or twice," he said, refusing to acknowledge her condescension. "You're not going to drown me, are you?" He grinned broadly.

Imani absorbed his smile but remained neutral. "We'll see."

She pushed the boat off the sand and jumped gracefully into position at the motor, a move she had perfected.

"Impressive," Diego said with a trace of sarcasm.

Imani didn't respond.

She took it slow through the inlet that led from the Wentworths' beach. Then, once in the river, she sped up and carved into a hard bend. Diego clung to the bench, and Imani noticed with satisfaction that his knuckles were white. *What a land monkey,* she thought.

As the boat emerged from the river into the turbulent channel, Diego twisted around to face her, his hands never leaving the bench. "Where are you taking me?"

Imani pointed to a low sandy mound ahead and to the left of them.

"Is that Chauncey Beach?" he shouted over the motor.

"Back side!" Imani shouted back. "Hold on." She sped up and headed straight for the beach, observing with pleasure the tension that rose through Diego's body as they accelerated. When his shoulders reached his ears, she cut the motor and let momentum and an incoming wave carry them toward the shore.

Diego's body relaxed gradually, and he turned to face her, his expression accusing.

"Safe and sound," she said.

"You're fucking nuts."

"You need a thesaurus."

When they hit sand, Imani gestured for Diego to get out, then watched in amusement as he angled his long legs over the bow with a little jump to avoid getting his boots wet. He was taller and leaner in his slim black jeans than she'd previously noticed. He looked out of place on the beach. Imani hopped out onto the damp sand and dragged the boat about eight feet from the waterline.

"Is it safe?" he asked.

Imani glanced around the empty beach. "From what? Clams?"

"From the tide, of course."

"I know the tides." Imani dropped the rope, then headed off down the shoreline.

Diego caught up with her, and they walked in silence for a while, with seagulls swooping and cawing overhead. The birds seemed unusually noisy, as if registering their suspicion of this stranger in black who clearly didn't belong there. Diego Landis belonged inside, Imani thought, with a book in his hands and a smug expression on his face. He belonged at Rita Mae's.

After a hundred yards, they came to a bend, around which was a clear view of the Atlantic. Imani stopped and stared into the infinite blue, feeling, as always, the pull of the tides. Her sneakers sank gently into the pale sand.

Diego stopped a few feet away and stared outward too, though whether that expanse of blue meant anything to him, Imani couldn't tell. The wind blew his hair straight across his face, forcing him to tuck it tightly behind his ears. After a few seconds, the wind won anyway. Imani dug out the rubber band she usually kept for Cady and held it out to him, but he shook his head.

"So where do we start?" he asked.

"I think you had some issues with my answers?" Imani sat in the cool dry sand, facing the water.

"Yes, I did, actually." He sat and pulled a piece of paper from his pocket. *"Whereas the unscored must merely accept what they are and muddle through life permanently flawed,"* he read, *"the scored receive monthly feedback from an impartial and highly intelligent source, which empowers us to change."*

"Wait." Imani looked at the neatly typed page. "You retyped all my answers?"

"No. Just the stupid ones," he said. "What makes you think the unscored can't change? Just because we don't have a software program judging us? We have parents. We get grades. We *are* equipped with brains. Remember those? We can figure out our flaws on our own if we want to."

"But where's your incentive to change?" Imani asked.

"Maybe some of us don't want to change," he said.

"Then I guess you go through life permanently flawed, like I said."

"Unlike you," he said. "Who get to—hold on—" He read from the piece of paper again. *"Achieve the contentedness of constant self-improvement."* He looked at Imani directly. "Jesus, are you even aware of how creepy that sounds?"

Imani had merely written out one of Score Corp's well-known slogans. "What's creepy about it?" she asked.

"For starters, the fact that it sounds like doublespeak?"

"What's doublespeak?"

He laughed sharply. "Unbelievable!" he said. "They introduce this massive mind control program; then they remove all references to mind control from the curriculum. *1984* used to be required reading. Did you know that?"

"Yeah, I've read that," Imani said, even though it wasn't true.

"So you *do* know what doublespeak is, then," he challenged.

She was beginning to feel outmatched but didn't want him to know that. "I've heard of it," she said.

"Right. So don't you think it's weird that we're living in Orwell's nightmare and we don't even read his book anymore?"

Imani knew she couldn't compete with Diego on the subject of a book she'd never read, so she tried to put the matter to rest. "Who cares about some stupid book?" she said. "All I know is I'm not living in anyone's nightmare."

"Yes, you are," Diego said. "The only thing Orwell got wrong was the bad guy. It's not the government. It's a corporation. A business, i.e., people making money. *A lot* of money. Do you even know about the history of Score Corp? Do you know about the controversy surrounding Sherry Potter's disappearance? Do you know about the lost interview?"

"Do you want me to answer any of these questions? Or are you just talking to yourself? Because if you'd rather talk to yourself, I'll go get my clam fork."

"Your *clam fork*?" Diego leaned forward and laughed. "What are you, a *clamdigger*?" His laughter expanded for a few seconds, then stopped suddenly like a choked motor. "Oh," he said.

Imani could see the dots connecting for him: *She has a boat,* he was thinking. *She knows the tides. Holy f%*#, she* is *a clamdigger!*

Diego reddened, and Imani knew she could have rescued

him with some kind of assurance, some casual display of magnanimity, but why would she do that when she could luxuriate in his discomfort? It was the perfect counterstrike to his previous crack about that book. How brilliant, she thought, that this intellectual *giant* with his holier-than-thou principles was a garden variety elitist.

"S-s-sorry . . . ," Diego stammered eventually. "I didn't mean to imply that . . . I mean, it's totally cool if you're a–"

"Save it," Imani said. "Just remember that I'm the one with the boat."

Diego's eyes widened. If Imani left him, he'd have to walk ten miles to the front side of Chauncey Beach, then another two to the nearest road, or attempt a shortcut through the unmarked dunes. Imani let him consider those options for a while. When he'd digested them, she drew a short line in the sand. "Round one to Imani LeMonde."

"Conceded." He let his left eye linger on hers, though whether it was to acknowledge his defeat or to demonstrate the magnanimity she had lacked, Imani couldn't tell. At any rate, the wind quickly made a shroud of his hair and he was forced to tuck it behind his ears again.

"So you were saying?" Imani began.

"Huh?"

"Some prattle about Sherry Potter's disappearance?"

"Oh, right. The lost interview. Do you know about it?"

Imani didn't.

"Okay," he said. "You know who Sherry Potter is, right?"

"Inventor of the score. With her husband, Nathan Klein."

"Right," he said. "So Sherry Potter gave one last interview before she disappeared. One interview where she completely discredited everything she and her husband did."

"I've never heard of that."

"It was destroyed," Diego said. "It never aired. And she hasn't been heard from since."

"How do you know it's real?"

"Search it," he said.

"Why?" Imani asked.

"Because if I were you, *that's* what I'd write my paper on."

"How is that 'opposing the score'?"

Diego rolled his eyes as if Imani were the thickest person in the universe. "Because Sherry Potter obviously believed her invention was a crime against humanity," he said. "Maybe you should find out why."

"Hmm," Imani said. She was aware of Sherry Potter's disappearance and of the rumors of her rift with Nathan Klein. It was potentially fertile ground for a paper opposing the score. "I'll think about it," she said. "In the meantime, I have some issues with *your* answers."

"I assumed you would." Diego smiled in anticipation.

"I didn't retype them because I have a life, but I recall you saying something about antisocial behavior being the only behavior worth defending?"

"Yeah," he said. "And just so you know, I retyped *your* answers because you have the handwriting of a psychopath."

Imani opened her mouth to object but ultimately couldn't. It was true. Her handwriting was an abomination. She had no patience for penmanship. She needed to record at the speed of thought and could type at lightning speed but hated even the feel of a pen in her hand. "Well, shouldn't you be defending my handwriting, then?"

"It's not antisocial," he said. "It's just sloppy."

"Well, that's why we have computers."

"Yeah. I'm sure that's why they were invented."

The wind, which seemed to have it in for Diego, plastered his hair across his face in a most undignified manner. Imani dug the rubber band out of her pocket and forced it into his hand. Reluctantly, he pulled his hair into a short ponytail. Without the curtain of hair, he looked different to Imani: angular and raw.

"What?" he said. "Why are you looking at me like that?"

Imani turned away and looked at the blue horizon, but with her peripheral vision she could see Diego grinning. He seemed to think he was winning whatever game they were playing. He was as sure of himself there at the back side of Chauncey Beach as he was in the classroom or at Rita Mae's. Where did that confidence come from? Was it the result of being rich, of knowing that no matter what you did or said, the world would open up for you? And what were his true motives toward Imani? Surely he didn't need that scholarship. Was he planning to turn her into a case study, as Ms. Wheeler suggested? Or was he merely toying with her? Whatever his motives, Imani felt compelled now to beat him. Whether it was an argument about some book or the scholarship itself, she wanted to win. She took a deep breath, then faced him. There was something animal-like about his jawline, but she refused to be intimidated by it.

"Forget about the stupid homework assignment," she said. "Tell me about your mother."

Suspicion flickered across the planes of his face. "My *mother?*" he asked.

Imani tried to remain poker-faced but was forced to turn away. She took a few deep salty breaths and reminded herself that she was on home turf here, that *Diego* was the outsider. Then she faced him with the most innocent expression she could muster under the circumstances. "Yeah," she said, "maybe I'll write my paper on *her.*"

Diego's eyes narrowed.

Imani forced a note of light flirtation into her tone. "I hear she knows even more about this anti-score stuff than you do."

Diego's blue eyes flashed with something like hostility. Then he turned away. "Sure," he said lightheartedly. "But if I were you, I'd look into Sherry Potter first."

"I can do that," Imani said, matching his lightness.

Then she too faced the ocean. She wanted to draw strength from it, but it offered none. The ocean was many things, but it was never sneaky, never dishonest. When it changed tacks, it was direct and merciless. When it placed you within its sights, it did so with a swagger Imani envied. She was on her own in this game. She'd have to find the strength to play it from within.

12. a more perfect humanity

IMANI DIDN'T BELIEVE in Sherry Potter's disappearance. It was impossible to disappear; there were cameras everywhere. Even if the press didn't know where Sherry Potter was, Imani was sure that Score Corp did, which meant her husband, Nathan Klein, did. Imani was also sure that the so-called lost interview was a conspiracy theory, hatched by creepers in lieu of a defensible argument for their cause. In any case, she decided not to debate the issue with Diego. She had a higher objective, and needed to draw him out to succeed. Even if she didn't end up writing her paper on Diego's mother, she had promised Ms. Wheeler and, more importantly, that eyeball that she'd uncover something useful.

So on Friday during study period, she claimed a tablet at the school library to search the lost interview, hoping to find just enough to show interest, butter Diego up, and then elicit some real information. Her search led her down blind alley after blind alley, with no actual "lost interview" appearing. The closest she got was a video of some girl who claimed to be Sherry Potter's assistant listening to a recording of it while describing what she heard. Before she could finish, someone barged into her dingy apartment and yanked her away. It looked amateurishly staged, which Imani found disappointing. She'd thought Diego was smarter than that and began to wonder if she'd mistaken his confidence for intelligence.

The search was not a complete loss for Imani, however. While there was no plausible evidence for the interview, there was an abundance of material about the Potter-Kleins themselves, and Imani quickly found herself spiraling down a search rabbit hole, consuming article after article about this oddball pair of geniuses. Her favorite bit was a ten-year-old interview with veteran reporter Martin Belzer. He was a star of news feeds and someone she knew her mother had a crush on. But he looked different in this interview younger, thinner, more aggressive.

The video featured footage of the Potter-Kleins' Cape Cod beach house, where they were shown riding horses while Martin Belzer provided a brief voice-over about the "reclusive couple" and their "world-changing software program." It explained how the Potter-Kleins had dropped out of MIT, cycled through a handful of startup companies, earned and lost a few million, and then finally designed the software at the heart of the score.

Their home was a sleek wooden deckhouse with eyeballs

everywhere. After a short tour, Martin sat with them in front of a digital fireplace to begin the inquisition.

The Potter-Kleins came across as friendly and open to Imani. Sherry was pretty and serious, with salt-and-pepper hair cut into a soft bob. Nathan was tall and gaunt with heavy black eyebrows and restless eyes. Despite being in their forties, they were both scored. They got a monthly report just like Imani did. Nathan's lowest score was 52, he admitted. Sherry had never scored below 80.

When Martin asked them why they invented the software, the Potter-Kleins looked at each other with a trace of trepidation.

Then Nathan answered: "We saw the inability of social programs, including public education, to eradicate poverty, and we decided it was a failure of technology."

"A failure of *technology*?" Martin asked.

"Of course," Nathan answered. "Here we had this incredible tool at our disposal with the Internet. We had search. We had wikis. We had all the social networking tools. We had micro-lending and personalized charity. But poverty wasn't going away. If anything, the Internet was widening the gap between rich and poor."

"The digital divide," Martin interjected.

"Sure, that," Nathan answered, "but also the fact that certain societal structures were being reinforced rather than challenged by the Internet. You know, poverty is not merely a question of resources. It's also a collection of behaviors."

"And that's not to blame the victim," Sherry interrupted. "Structural economic issues certainly have their role."

"Yes," Nathan conceded. "But behavioral patterns reinforce inequities because people tend to behave according to the dictates of whatever value system they're born into. And the value systems of the poor tend to reinforce poverty. High birth rates, high drop-out rates, short-term versus delayed gratification."

"All excellent replicators," Sherry added.

"It's a runaway feedback loop," Nathan continued. "A self-replicating pattern. And no one found a way to stop it. *No one.*"

"Okay," Martin said, "so you're telling me you were looking for a way to . . ."

"To interrupt the pattern," Nathan said.

"But first," Sherry added, "we had to understand it."

"Exactly," Nathan said. "So we created a software program that could crunch huge quantities of data in search of the nonobvious patterns."

"We already knew the obvious ones," Sherry said.

"Exactly," Nathan agreed. "And it's really just blind luck that this all happened around the same time that surveillance cameras were cropping up everywhere."

The way they spoke seemed to Imani like a duet between a guitar and a piano, overlapping at times but always complementing.

"Our software could identify subjects through biometric markers," Sherry said. "Like face and gait recognition. But now we could link that data with things like Web usage and direct address."

"Direct address?" Martin asked.

"That's when people speak directly to the cameras," she said.

"Of course," Martin said. "That's one of the aspects of the score that makes people—especially people of our generation—very uncomfortable."

"Yes, I know," Sherry said. "It makes a lot of people uncomfortable. Luckily, we found a juvenile detention facility in New Hampshire that wasn't uncomfortable with it."

"At *all*," Nathan interjected.

"Exborough," Martin said, nodding.

Sherry and Nathan looked at each other for a grim moment, until Martin prodded them. "Things didn't exactly go as planned at Exborough," he said. "Did they?"

"There were some bumps along the way," Nathan offered.

"Bumps?" Martin waited for them to expand, but they did not. "The records from Exborough are all sealed," he said finally. "Along with your research notes."

"Our subjects were minors," Sherry explained gently. "They have certain legal protections."

"They're not minors anymore," Martin pushed. "What can you tell us?"

In the silence that followed, the camera zoomed in, first on Nathan, who remained impassive, then on Sherry, whose jaw tensed.

This seemed to stiffen Martin's resolve. "Why won't you tell us what happened at Exborough?"

Nathan turned to Sherry, and it seemed to Imani that something transpired between them, an agreement of some kind.

"Look," Sherry said. "You have to remember, these were troubled kids. Long before we came along, there was drug use, violence, theft. There was *organized* crime and prostitution. *At the facility.* The authorities were at their wits' end. So were the parents, in most cases. I think that's how they justified it."

"Is that how *you* justified it?" Martin asked.

"We were invited," Nathan said.

"You were invited to put those kids under twenty-four-hour surveillance?" Martin challenged.

Sherry smiled patiently. "They were already under surveillance," she said.

"Look," Nathan continued, "we were just looking for a way to feed massive amounts of data into our software. Exborough was perfectly set up *already* for that purpose. We were going to toss all the data afterward."

"It was the kids themselves who changed our minds," Sherry said. "I remember the day the warden called to tell us they were confessing to the cameras." She turned to her husband, laughing. "Do you remember that?"

Nathan nodded.

"Confessing?" Martin asked, incredulous.

Sherry nodded. "It was so strange. We never anticipated it. We hoped the kids would get used to the cameras and maybe ignore them after a while. But something else happened. The kids loved the cameras; they loved being watched! I remember thinking it was probably because it was a kind of micro-celebrity. You know, like the old reality TV."

Martin wrinkled his nose in distaste.

"That was my reaction too," Sherry said. "But you have to remember, these kids were already used to being watched."

"All kids are," Nathan said. "That's the salient point here. That was our lightbulb moment."

"What do you mean by that?" Martin asked.

"Even before the score," Nathan said. "Before Exborough, before the first closed-circuit camera was installed in the first convenience store, being a kid has always been about being watched. They're watched by their parents, by their teachers, by each other. Look at a baby. All it *wants* is to be watched. It cries when you look away. Look at little kids on the play-ground: 'Mommy, Mommy, look at me.'"

"But the older we get," Sherry continued, "the less we look at each other. Watch commuters on a train. Nobody makes eye contact. The checkout girl at the supermarket? Do you ever look her in the eye?"

Martin laughed in a self-deprecating manner.

"And, on a macro scale, look at what's happened to our communities," Nathan said. "We used to live in small clusters, in tiny villages. Do you think there was any privacy there? There were no fenced-off backyards. There were no locks on the doors. Everyone knew everyone else's business."

"Right," Sherry said. "For thousands of years, that's how we lived. That's our natural heritage. Our human nature, if you will."

"But as communities grew in size," Nathan said, "so did the fetishization of privacy."

"The *fetishization* of privacy," Martin said, clearly disturbed by the phrase.

"Privacy is a modern invention," Nathan said. "There's no hardwired need for it. If anything, the opposite is true."

"Yes," Sherry continued, "and, interestingly, this cultural evolution toward privacy is precisely mirrored on an individual scale. The baby who craves attention becomes the adult who doesn't know her own neighbors. The child who begged his mommy to look at him on the playground becomes the sullen teenager who locks his bedroom door and puts up a KEEP OUT sign. Where does he learn this?" She paused to let the question hang, before answering: "From his parents."

"And from society," Nathan added.

"But the kids at Exborough were different," Sherry said with a warm smile, leaning in toward Martin. "They were alienated from their parents and from society. Not to mention, because of where they were, privacy was already dead for them." She leaned farther forward, as if to share a secret. "We had no way of knowing this beforehand, but these kids were primed for this experiment. The cameras tapped into something primal for them. I think it reawakened something."

"What do you think it awakened?" Martin asked.

Sherry stared into the camera for a long moment, then said: "Faith."

"Faith in what?"

"Fair play," Sherry said.

Martin cocked his head to the side, awaiting clarification.

"They knew they were being judged," she explained. "I mean, to be honest, we didn't know if the software would work in the beginning. But the kids knew their behavior was being evaluated somehow. It didn't bother them. They were used to being judged. Only now, instead of being judged by a frustrated teacher, or a potentially abusive guard, or by a disapproving parent, they were being judged by something rational, something fair. Something not human."

"Exactly," Nathan said with great satisfaction.

"And they liked this?" Martin asked. "The nonhuman aspect?" Martin's tone was pinched, as if he found the concept profoundly offensive.

"Humans had failed these kids time and time again," Sherry said. "I think for a lot of them, this was the first time they'd ever been judged fairly."

"By a software program." Martin's face again betrayed his discomfort with the idea.

"By the most intelligent software program ever created," Nathan said.

Sherry gave her husband a sidelong glance.

But Nathan was uncowed. "Hey, you can't argue with the results. On every measurable parameter—income, health, marital stability, educational level, quality of life—the score's predictive capacity is off the charts."

Sherry grew quiet in the face of her husband's grandstanding.

"A more perfect humanity through technology," Martin said, quoting Score Corp's well-known slogan.

"That's right," Nathan said. "Where sociology, criminology,

psychology, and, to be quite frank, all of the humanities have failed, the score has finally succeeded."

"But is that a worthy goal?" Martin asked.

"What?" Nathan said. "Perfection?"

"Exactly," Martin said. "To a lot of people, that sounds frighteningly utopian."

Nathan leaned forward threateningly. "What are you afraid of, Martin?"

Taken aback by the direct confrontation, Martin shook his head and jowls in the exaggerated manner that Imani recognized from more recent news feeds. "I'm not afraid of anything," he backtracked. "But I think a lot of people—"

"A lot of people were perfectly happy to subject their children to the SATs and to all manner of standardized tests," Nathan interrupted. "Let's look at the SAT. All it had to do was predict an incoming college freshman's academic performance. Do you want to know how accurate those predictions really were? Seventeen percent. *Seventeen* percent! That means four out of five times, it was completely wrong. Yet colleges relied on it, and billions were spent keeping this unequivocal failure of a social experiment not merely alive but *central* to the lives of young people. Why? Because it had the illusion of neutrality, and of science." He took a breather and looked at his wife.

"Yeah, but Nathan," Sherry said, "the real reason it was kept alive is even worse."

"What's that?" Martin asked, his thick eyebrows furrowing.

"Because the SAT was easily gamed," Sherry said. "If you

could afford one of those test-prep courses, you could just buy yourself a higher score. The SAT was a way for rich people to pretend their children were *gifted,* when, in fact, they were just privileged."

"Exactly," Nathan said.

"And how is the score different?" Martin asked.

"You can't game it," Sherry said.

"Why?" Martin asked.

"The software learns from the attempt," she said. "It's just more feedback to make it smarter."

"How smart?" Martin asked.

"Smarter than us," Nathan said, grinning. "And we're pretty smart."

Sherry gave Nathan another sidelong glare, then looked back at Martin. "The thing to remember about the score is that, at its heart, it's not so much about *what you do.* It's about *who you are.*"

"And there's no test-prep course for that," Nathan said.

"No," Sherry added. "Just the hard work of honest self-improvement."

"Is *that* what people are afraid of?" Nathan asked smugly.

Imani had headphones on, so she missed the bell when it rang. It was only the parade of students exiting the library that pulled her attention from the screen. With reluctance, she closed the window, and walked out of the library with Nathan Klein's last words resonating in her mind: *Is* that *what people are afraid of?*

Imani sat through English class, taking cursory notes, but

her thoughts remained with the Potter-Kleins. There wasn't much for *her* to use from that interview, but it was a potential treasure trove for Diego.

Imani had never given much thought to the Potter-Kleins before. If asked, she would have said they were a couple of computer geeks. But now she saw that they were so much more: they were visionaries. And what was wrong with having a utopian vision for humanity? Only a cynic would criticize them for it. If technology could help the human race get closer to perfection, where was the harm in it? Were human beings so admirable in their natural state?

Imani replayed her favorite moment in her mind, when Nathan got all serious and said: "What are you afraid of, Martin?" It was a perfect line to use on Diego.

After English class, she found another note from him in her locker.

Meet me in the alley behind the ice rink on Saturday at noon. I want to show you Chauncey Beach my way. I'll take care of the subterfuge.

D. Landis, Thesaurus Needer

Imani pocketed the note, thrilled at the opportunity to fire that winning line at him.

13. twit

ON SATURDAY AFTERNOON, when Imani emerged from the ice rink into the back alley, Diego was already there. He leaned against his scooter reading a paperback called *Conquer the Five Elements in Five Easy Steps.*

"Those books are a waste of time," Imani said.

Diego shook his head as he flipped through the pages. "I don't know. According to this, you'd have to go out of your way *not* to be a high ninety." He snapped the book shut. "Take off your coat and shoes."

"Excuse me?"

Diego opened the trunk of his scooter and pulled out a long black coat and some black lace-up boots. He handed them to Imani, who examined them with disdain.

"They're my mother's," he said.

"Is your mother a vampire?"

"According to some." Diego reached back into the trunk, then handed her a shiny black helmet. "With these on," he said, "you could be anyone. Even a filthy unscored like me."

Imani considered telling Diego that she'd already confessed their collaboration to the software so there was no need for the disguise. But she decided against it. If he thought she was taking a terrible risk to be with him, perhaps he'd be more likely to reveal sensitive information. She put on his mother's coat and boots, then slid into the helmet.

Diego straddled his scooter and waited for her to climb on behind him, but Imani hesitated.

"I'm a safe driver," he said. "I've only crashed once. But it was the other guy's fault."

It wasn't the scooter Imani was afraid of. She'd spent the past two years on the back of Cady's, which was like being tethered to a gale force wind. It was the memory of Malachi Beene that frightened her. It was because of him that she'd sworn off *all* physical contact with boys. And now here was Diego, his long legs hugging the scooter, his straight back waiting for her to press herself against it. There was nothing inherently sexual about riding behind someone on a scooter, but she wished Diego had a car, something with a wide front seat, seat belts, and a lot of room between passenger and driver.

Imani took a moment to remind herself why she was there, why it was worth the risk. Then she approached the scooter and climbed on behind Diego. There was no rear bar to hang on to, just the rounded trunk, which she clung to awkwardly.

"You all right back there?" Diego asked.

"Just go," she said.

Diego started down the alley. Imani scooted as far back as possible, leaving a gap between them wide enough for a third rider.

Diego was a much safer driver than Cady, who tended to treat all other vehicles as competitors or obstacles. They turned from the Causeway into the hinterlands of Somerton, past St. James College and the nature preserve. Dozens of eyeballs ticked by overhead, but with the long black coat and obliterating helmet, Imani was invisible to them, a thought that made her stomach flutter with both excitement and guilt.

The road to Chauncey Beach was mostly empty, curving gracefully beneath the canopy of budding trees. It was a five-mile ride to the end, and the parking lot was closed for the off-season, as marked by a handwritten sign bolted to a swing gate. Diego swerved easily around it, then headed toward the shuttered hamburger stand. Stuck like lollipops throughout the parking lot were a handful of light poles with eyeballs dangling from them.

"Hold on!" he shouted.

In imitation of Imani's expert beaching of Frankenwhaler a few days earlier, he sped up and juddered his scooter over the lip of the boardwalk. Swaying roughly, Imani had no choice but to squeeze his hips with her knees. As the wooden planks jolted them upward, she refused to hold on to his waist, suspecting that such an indignity was precisely his intention.

Diego paused briefly at the top to tease her with a glimpse of the broad beach and glistening Atlantic, then he turned right and rode into the dunes.

Imani rarely ventured into the dunes herself. She preferred the waterline. She knew there were no eyeballs beyond a certain point, which meant lowbies went to the dunes to conduct themselves in the manner of lowbies. She wasn't sure what Diego did there, and the prospect of learning this made her stomach flutter even more.

They descended into some trees, then followed the boardwalk over a network of streams. The interior of the dunes was surprisingly lush. Vines, bushes, and even some noisy insects fleshed out the parched surroundings into an unlikely Eden. They rode alone and unwatched through the shady network until a rise in the boardwalk brought them out of the trees and back to the bright white of the dunes. The ocean could be neither seen nor heard. After another ten minutes, the boardwalk ended abruptly. There, about fifteen scooters and a handful of bikes lay haphazardly in the sand as if spit up by the boardwalk itself.

Leaving his scooter among the others, Diego followed a riot of footprints up the side of a high dune. "Come on," he said. "We have to climb."

Imani followed him to the top, where he looked downward. "Behold," he said. "The pit."

Down below, it was, indeed, a pit. About twenty yards by fifty yards and perimetered by high dunes, it had been carved by the wind. At the bottom, about twenty kids milled about, some drinking beer, some tending to a small fire in the center.

Diego grabbed Imani's hand while starting down the steep side. Imani pulled roughly away from him. He stopped his descent and faced her.

"Sorry," he said. "It's just that it's steep."

"I'm okay," she said. She dug her heels into the soft sand and descended the steep side on her own. Before long, the steepness forced her to run, then jump. Diego followed behind her at a respectable distance. Once at the bottom, she looked around at all of the unfamiliar faces. Diego walked up behind her.

"Are they all unscored?" she whispered.

Diego nodded.

She didn't recognize any of them from Somerton High. "How do you know them?" she asked.

"A software program forces us to be friends," he said.

"Ha-ha," she said flatly.

"Actually, most of them are from my old school." He waved to a cluster of girls sitting on a felled tree, roasting marshmallows in the fire. One of them, a tall girl with dark hair pulled into a tight ponytail, came over to greet them.

"Hey, Diego," she said. "Who's your friend?" Without waiting for an answer, she extended her hand to Imani with a dazzling smile that reminded her of Ms. Wheeler. "I'm Erica."

Imani had spent most of her life avoiding the unscored. When she hesitated, the girl dropped her hand and let her eyes wander down Imani's strange outfit.

"It's a disguise," Diego said. "She doesn't usually dress like that."

"Oh my God. You're *scored*?" Erica whispered the word "scored," but in a way that managed to make it louder. "No, no, no. That's great. I'm *so* glad you came." Her face filled with kindness and a hint of pity that made Imani uncomfortable. "You're, like, completely welcome here," she said.

"Thanks, Erica," Diego said. He guided Imani away. "Don't mind her," he said under his breath. "She gets all excited when she meets the scored."

"Why?" Imani asked.

"She thinks she can rescue them or something," Diego mumbled, as if he were embarrassed.

Erica returned to her cluster of friends but continued gesturing toward Imani with an aura of good intentions that felt patronizing.

"I didn't realize I needed rescuing," Imani said.

Diego sat on a felled tree near the fire. "You wouldn't, though, would you?"

Imani sat next to him. After the exchange with Erica—she'd never met a *friendly* unscored—she took comfort in the protocol of insults she and Diego had established. "So what is this?" She glanced around at the assortment of strangers, some with longish hair like Diego's, some in the sloppy style of the local rich kids. "A secret hideout?"

"Yeah," he said. "We come here to engage in antisocial behavior while plotting the downfall of society."

"I thought society had already fallen."

"It's sick," he said. "But it's still standing."

"And what's your strategy to bring it down?"

"You'll see," he said. "Now, can we cut the crap, please, and get down to business? I need a thesis for *my* paper. I gave you yours."

"Fine," Imani said. She was equally eager to begin extracting information from him. "Why don't you explore the philosophy behind the score?"

"What? Total mind control and world domination?" Diego asked.

"I was thinking more along the lines of 'a more perfect humanity through technology.'"

Diego leaned away from her. "Are you kidding me?"

"What? You don't think that's a worthy goal?"

Diego narrowed his eyes at her in an expression that seemed to say, *You are vastly strange and a little scary.* It was, of course, intended as an insult, but Imani didn't mind it. She enjoyed being unfathomable to Diego. As he continued to stare at her, she prepared to unleash Nathan Klein's line on him.

But Diego stole the moment. "It's code," he said.

Imani was thrown off. "What's code?"

"'A more perfect humanity through technology,'" he said. "It's code for eliminating the unscored."

"Says who?"

"We're a glitch in their program," he said. "What Score Corp wants is to make the entire human race as predictable and controllable as machines."

"That's ridiculous," Imani scoffed.

"You're calling me ridiculous?" His face was totally flat.

"How about paranoid?" Imani amended.

Diego chuckled dismissively, then poked at the sand with a stick.

"Oh, come on," Imani prodded. "You're saying the whole point of the score is to oppress *you*? Don't you think that's a little self-centered?"

Diego threw his head back and squinted against the sun, a mocking smile on his face. "You're so naive."

"And you're an overblown twit!"

"Whoa!" He faced her, still smiling. "*Twit?* Really?" He picked up the tiny stick and broke it in half. "Did you get that from your thesaurus?"

Imani looked away, annoyed.

"Or is that what you're stuck with because the software prohibits swearing?" Diego asked.

"It fits," Imani said. "And the software doesn't *prohibit* swearing."

"So say 'fuck.' Say 'fuck, fuck, fuck.'"

Imani stared at him coldly.

"See?" he said. "You can't do it. Can you?"

"I *can* do it. I choose not to."

"Oh, of course. Because it's a violation . . . of what? Impulse control?"

Rapport, actually, Imani thought, but she wasn't interested in a debate on the fitness of swearing.

"Fine, I'm a twit then," he said. "You know what you are?"

Imani braced herself. He'd probably rehearsed something.

Diego leaned forward and brought his lips to her ear. "You're beautiful," he whispered.

"Rangers!" It was a young boy, around thirteen, standing at the top of a dune. Everyone at the bottom of the pit froze. Then, hearing the buzz in the distance, they all jumped into action.

Diego was off the felled tree at the first warning. He grabbed Imani's hand and yanked her up the steep incline of the dune. Imani pulled free of him instinctively but struggled to get up the side. It was like climbing up a sugar bowl. When Diego reached back again for her, she took his hand and let him pull her upward.

"You're not supposed to be here, are you?" she asked as they climbed.

"Nope," he said. "All the inland dunes beyond the boardwalk are off-limits."

When they got to the top, she pulled her hand free of his. "So what are you doing here?" she asked.

"Being antisocial?" he offered. He headed to the boardwalk and joined the others scrambling to get their bikes and scooters upright. When he had righted his, he removed one helmet and threw it to Imani. "Are you ready for some fun?"

Imani caught the helmet but didn't move.

Diego straddled his scooter, put on his own helmet, and waited for her, while the others took off down the boardwalk in a melee of sand and sound. "You can stay if you want to," Diego said over the noise. "But the rangers will turn you in to the police."

"And you know this because?"

He flashed her that devious smile, then revved his scooter.

Imani put on the helmet and joined him on the scooter, convinced she'd made a terrible—and irreversible—mistake by going there with him. Diego lurched for the boardwalk, then sped to catch up with the others, passing several within seconds. Imani squeezed Diego's hips with her knees. In the rush to escape, she hadn't thought about Diego's whispered words, but they returned now, mixing themselves into the adrenaline rush of flight. She pushed back from Diego to leave room for the phantom third rider, and gripped the trunk with both hands. The scooter wobbled over the boards, nearly knocking her off. Diego reached back with one hand, grabbed her arm, and pulled her closer to him. She had no choice but to plaster herself to his back and wrap her arms around his waist for the rest of the rough ride. Silently, she vowed to make him pay for the indignity.

After a minute, the long line of scooters stopped and bunched up as people in the front yelled back at them. Imani couldn't hear what they were saying, so she stood on Diego's pedals and spotted the black three-wheeled ATV of a Chauncey Beach ranger up ahead.

"Hold on," Diego said. He shouted at the people behind them to turn around.

The boardwalk was less than five feet wide, and his words launched a near-disastrous rotation of bikes and scooters. Diego and Imani came within inches of tumbling off the edge as Diego turned his scooter in four arcs. He was no Cady Fazio,

Imani thought. Cady would have had Frankenscooter turned around and out of there in no time flat.

Up ahead, two scooters fell off the boardwalk and made their way through the underbrush, sending pinwheels of sand into the faces of their friends.

"Where are we going?" Imani shouted over the roar.

Diego didn't answer. When the boardwalk ended, he launched straight into the sand. For a moment, she feared he would take them down into the pit. She clung to his waist in anticipation. But instead of taking them down, he pulled in front of the others and led the whole pack away from the pit and over the lower dunes. Before long, they were heading down the broad beach toward the water. Hogg Island loomed in the distance. Bearings gained, Imani realized they were at the back of Chauncey Beach, not far from where she had taken Diego by boat.

Diego leaned over the handlebars as he sped for the shoreline. Imani put her head on his back, clasped one hand around her other wrist, and tried to breathe. The ocean sped by them on the right, and on their left, faster scooters caught up, then overtook them. The kids on bikes had to carry them down the dunes, but once they hit firm sand, they pedaled furiously.

At the top of one of the dunes was a green-clad ranger, standing on the pedals of his ATV. Though she knew some of the Chauncey Beach rangers, she didn't recognize him. They were mostly 70s and hailed from Somerton and the surrounding area. One of them, Tara Luboff, had been her babysitter when she was a kid. Imani dreaded being caught on the back of an unscored's scooter by the girl who used to make her burnt popcorn. The ranger at the top of the dune spoke calmly into a unit on his wrist, then, after watching the line of bikes and scooters flee, he disappeared into the dunes.

It was a long ride down the shoreline. Chauncey Beach stretched for ten miles from the back to the parking lot. The rangers didn't pursue them; they didn't have to. The only way off the beach was through the parking lot. All they had to do was wait there.

Up ahead, two kids peeled off from the pack and headed through the soft sand back up to the dunes.

"Hold on," Diego shouted over his shoulder. Then he too peeled off and followed the kids up the dunes.

They picked up the boardwalk again and followed for a while until Diego stopped suddenly. He planted his feet on either side and twisted around to face Imani.

"Here's the drill," he said.

Imani began to lift her visor, but he put his hand over hers, then pointed to an eyeball in the trees. It was overgrown with vines, but there were probably others. They must have been close to the parking lot.

Imani secured her visor. "You have a *drill*?"

"Yeah, it's a game we play with the rangers. How it works is a few of us meet them in the parking lot and lead them into the woods toward Manor Hill while the others head home."

"And then what happens?"

"Well, then we hope the Chaunceys don't release the dogs."

"*What?*"

"The rangers are pussies," he said. "They won't go very far onto the Chaunceys' private property."

"Because of the dogs," Imani said. She was aware of the Chaunceys' infamous Dobermans. "What an excellent drill. What a meaningful way to spend your weekend. First you despoil a pristine dune with your fire and beer cans. Then you—"

"They have no right declaring those dunes off-limits," Diego said, his voice rising in anger. "Who the hell are they to decide where we can and can't go? What is this, a police state?"

"That's a little dramatic, don't you think?"

"You're so naive."

"Yeah, I think we covered that earlier. And they're not the police. They work for the Fish and Wildlife Department."

"So?" he said. "Do they own the sand? Do they own the air?"

"They don't *own* anything," Imani said. "These are public lands. They're just trying to protect them."

"Well, I don't acknowledge their right to do that," he said. "I think it's bullshit that some government agency can just declare a piece of the world off-limits. They let hunters roam through here to shoot deer."

Imani shook her head. "That's for population control."

"I knew *that*," he said. But the defensiveness in his tone told Imani he hadn't.

"Just get me out of here," she said.

He faced front and lurched the scooter forward punishingly. Imani's knees tightened around his hips, but she did not put her arms around him again.

Up ahead, the two other kids sat up on their parked scooters, waving for Diego to stop. Diego cut the engine and walked it the rest of the way toward them. Where the boardwalk ended, there was a small hill that led right down to the parking lot. The exit was less than twenty yards to the left.

"Let's do it now," the girl said. "Before the others get here."

"I'm not going with you," Diego said. He gestured toward Imani with his head.

"Three scooters are better than two," the girl said. "If the rangers think they have a shot at pulling us down, they'll chase us farther into the woods."

"I have to get her out of here," he said.

"Why?" The girl looked Imani up and down. "What's so special about her?"

Imani could only make out the girl's eyes, in the opening of her helmet, smudged in bright blue eyeliner with yellow mascara. The unscored often dressed bizarrely, as if to accentuate their outcast status, a habit Imani had never understood.

"I just do," Diego said.

He and Imani got off, then he pushed the scooter as gently as possible down the low hill, almost losing control on a patch of beach grass. About a hundred yards away, the two rangers, one male, one female, sat on their ATVs facing the burger stand where they expected the other scooters to arrive any minute via the boardwalk. The gentle purring of their motors covered Diego and Imani's retreat.

They were yards away from the exit, moments from a clean getaway, when the two kids they'd left behind came barreling down the hill at top speed. When the rangers spotted them charging across the parking lot, they saw Diego and Imani too.

Diego scrambled onto the scooter, and Imani slid on right behind him. Diego skidded a 180 on a patch of sand until they were facing an oncoming ranger. She wore a helmet, so Imani couldn't tell if it was Tara Luboff. As the ranger sped toward them, Diego attempted to turn the scooter around rather than powering his way out of the jam.

"Don't you know how to ride this thing?" Imani yelled. She was trying to calculate just how many points she'd lose for being arrested when an incredible sight stole all of her attention.

Behind the advancing ranger, beyond the burger stand, three scooters crested the top of a dune with a fantail of sand, then nose-dived into the parking lot at full speed. Another one followed. Then another and another. While Diego and Imani careened inelegantly around the exit gate to make for Chauncey Beach Road, they overtook the female ranger and crisscrossed in front of her. A steady pulse of bikes and scooters came screaming down the boardwalk. Joining the others, they harassed the ranger like a swarm of wasps.

Imani twisted around to watch as the ranger stopped short. The last thing she saw as Diego sped down Chauncey Beach Road was the ranger grabbing a girl by the elbow and tearing her from her bicycle. Imani gasped. Both the girl and her bike were still airborne when a bend in the road tore them from Imani's sight. The savagery of the ranger's act, along with the fact that it *might* have been her former babysitter, horrified her.

Diego sped down Chauncey Beach Road, his scooter straining to reach its maximum speed. At some point, she wasn't sure when, Imani had let go of the trunk and clung to Diego's waist, her right hand clamped over her left wrist.

Now that they were on smooth asphalt, Imani let go and held on to the trunk again. Eventually, Diego's friends appeared beside them, gathering into a single line until one of them took the lead. Once they were safely out of the rangers' jurisdiction, they all streamed into the parking lot of an ice cream stand, still shuttered for the off-season.

Diego stopped, then told Imani to wait while he joined the others dismounting their scooters to gather in shifting huddles. Imani kept her visor down but gathered from the discussions that the rangers had gotten a girl and a guy. They were hurt but not severely. One girl, who seemed older than the rest, possibly college-aged, stood apart from the others to make a call. She had black-and-white-striped hair and wore a short black skirt with tall black boots. She rejoined her friends and assured them all that "wheels were turning." When the others returned to their scooters, the girl walked with Diego back to his.

"Foundation, Wednesday," she told him. "Do not be late this time."

"I'm never late," he said.

"You're *always* late."

"No," he said. "*You* always start too early."

Imani got off the scooter so that Diego could get on. The girl with the black-and-white hair gave her a quick glance, then walked away to her own scooter.

"Who's she?" Imani asked.

"No one."

As Diego turned right to head into the town of Somerton, Imani began to wonder if the gathering at the pit had a political purpose. Was it possible they had set the fire to draw out the rangers? Were they hoping to be arrested? Were those the "wheels" that were turning?

Diego pulled into the alley behind the ice rink and stopped by the door. He didn't cut the motor. He waited while Imani climbed off.

"So what I said back there at the pit?" he said. "You know, about you being . . ." He rolled his eyes. "Beautiful?"

"Yeah?" she said.

"I was just messing with you," he said.

"Sure, whatever." She took off the helmet and handed it to him. "So what's the foundation? That girl with the striped hair told you not to be late for it."

"It's nothing."

Imani gave him his mother's coat and sat down on the concrete steps to unlace her boots. "How can you be late for nothing?" she asked.

"You don't want to know," he said. "Believe me."

"What if I do?"

Diego rolled his scooter back onto its stand and watched her take the boots off.

"What?" she said. "You think I can't handle it, whatever it is?"

He laughed. "It's the *Chaos* Foundation," he said. "But I don't think it's your kind of thing." He reached back to get Imani's own coat and boots from the trunk, then tossed them to her. "So you're not mad at me?"

Imani wanted to press him for more details about the Chaos Foundation, but she detected a distinct unwillingness to divulge them, and she didn't want to raise suspicion.

"Mad about what?" she asked, shoving her feet into her own boots. "Being recklessly endangered by someone who can barely drive a scooter?"

"Excuse me, but I'm an excellent driver."

"Oh, really, I couldn't tell." She stood up and shrugged into her coat. "So you must have been referring to your offer to feed me to the Chaunceys' Dobermans?"

"I was referring to my calling you beautiful."

"Yeah, what an insult."

"It made you blush," he said, smiling broadly.

"Black girls don't blush."

"Your mother's white."

"How do you know that?"

"Is it supposed to be a secret?"

"No," she said. "But I don't know much about *your* mother."

"She's highly searchable," he said. "And you *did* blush."

"I was embarrassed," she said. "For you." She pulled her thick braid out of the collar of her coat.

"So anyway," Diego said, "I still don't have a topic."

"I've already given you several topics."

"Several?"

"*Several*. And what have you given me? A conspiracy theory about Sherry Potter's disappearance."

"She's still missing."

Imani reached for the door handle behind her. "Yeah, well, this whole collaboration is off unless you give me something I can use."

Diego rolled his eyes upward. "Do you really want to write about my mother?" he asked.

Imani kept her hand on the door handle. "Depends on what you tell me. A lot of people think she's a crackpot."

"So now you're *insulting* my mother."

"Well, she does dress like a vampire."

"*You* dress like a clamdigger."

"Thank you," Imani said. "And it's *clammer*."

"Of course," he said. "My mistake."

"I'll pick the next meeting place," she said.

"Okay, *clammer*."

Imani searched for an equivalent comeback but nothing came to mind, other than "twit," which, in retrospect, she had to agree was inadequate. "Let's not do cutesy nicknames," she said.

Diego was cocking his head to the side as he looked at her, appraisingly. "Do you ever wear your hair down?"

"Do I ever—" She stopped herself when she realized he was probably messing with her again. "No," she revised. Then she opened the door and went inside.

Through the door, she could hear his laughter for a moment, then the hum of his scooter as it carried him away.

14. "we"

there was a note in Imani's locker.

The Chaos Foundation cannot be described with mere words. It must be experienced live. If you're game, come to Abate Hall at St. James College at 10 on Wednesday night. It's an eyeball-free zone. Notice I didn't say "safe zone." I'm learning. Oh, and sorry I made that comment about your hair, but you had it coming.

Diego L., Chaos Facilitator

When Imani looked up from the note, her classmates were filing past her on their way to homeroom. She put the note in her pocket, closed her locker, and went straight to the principal's office.

Ms. Wheeler read the note while Imani stood in her

doorway. The late bell rang. "Don't worry about homeroom," Ms. Wheeler said. "I'll get you excused. Come in and close the door."

Imani did as she was told and sat down.

Ms. Wheeler put the note on her desk, unfurled her tap pad, and started typing. "It doesn't look like they have a website."

"Maybe it's an alias?" Imani ventured.

Ms. Wheeler's specs flashed with data as she typed. "Yeah, all I'm getting are some references to an Isaac Asimov novel." She blinked away her display to look at Imani. "Is he into science fiction? Don't tell me I'm going to have to read Isaac Asimov."

Imani shrugged. "I don't really know what he's into."

Ms. Wheeler examined the note. "Chaos facilitator," she said. "I don't like the sound of *that*. Is it a student group? Do you know if any adults are involved?"

"All I know is that this other girl is involved. Someone I've never seen before. I didn't get her name, but she has black-and-white-striped hair."

"A high school girl?"

"I'm not sure," Imani said. "Maybe college?"

Ms. Wheeler looked suspicious. "And how exactly did you meet this girl?"

Imani hesitated. She hadn't intended to tell Ms. Wheeler about the incident in the dunes. Soliciting information from an unscored was one thing. Nearly getting arrested was something else. But Ms. Wheeler seemed to know she was withholding something, and Imani didn't want to squander the trust she'd already established with her.

"Diego took me to Chauncey Beach this weekend," she said finally. "And we sort of got chased out of the dunes."

"Chased?" Ms. Wheeler looked worried. "By whom? By the police?"

Imani shook her head. "Just the beach rangers." She went on to tell Ms. Wheeler the whole story, including her tentative theory that Diego and his friends might have set the fire for the purpose of drawing out the rangers.

"This girl with the black-and-white hair," Imani said. "She was on her cell with someone, and she said, 'Wheels are turning.'"

"Wheels are turning." Ms. Wheeler sat back in her chair and swiveled.

"Yeah," Imani continued. "And she told Diego not to be late for that meeting on Wednesday."

Ms. Wheeler looked at the note again. "This meeting at St. James College?"

Imani nodded. She could tell by Ms. Wheeler's close attention to her every word that she had delivered something potentially useful. "What do you think it is?" she asked.

Ms. Wheeler inspected the note. "I'd hate to even speculate," she said.

"Well, I'll pay close attention at the meeting," Imani promised.

"Oh, no." Ms. Wheeler shook her head. "I don't want you

anywhere near that meeting. You've done enough already. You just leave this with me."

"But I thought—"

Another shake of Ms. Wheeler's head concluded the discussion. Imani wanted to appeal, but Ms. Wheeler rose and opened the door. "Sally," she said to Mrs. Bronson, standing behind the reception desk. "Get Pulaski for me, will you?"

Mrs. Bronson nodded.

Imani got up and went to the door. "Is that Chief Pulaski?"

Ms. Wheeler waved a finger at her. "Let's just keep this quiet," she said. "Don't bring up the subject with Diego again, okay? Let them have their meeting. We'll take it from here."

"We?" Imani asked.

In place of an answer, Ms. Wheeler offered a warm smile. "Well done, Imani. This could be extremely useful." She held up the note. "And I'm sure you'll be rewarded for it."

Imani's mood soared. "Really? You're sure?"

"Absolutely." Ms. Wheeler was already walking back to her desk. "Shut the door on your way out, will you?"

Imani stood and watched her for a moment longer, wanting to soak up the promise of a reward from Score Corp, but Ms. Wheeler had disappeared once again behind the flashing lights of her specs.

"We're talking about the collapse of the middle class," Mr. Carol said. He was especially riled up that day, sitting on top of the desk that divided the scored from the unscored, his elbows resting on his knees. The weekend must have recharged his outrage battery, Imani thought.

"The American dream was never about getting rich," he said. "It was about poor people coming here to be middle class. A decent home, a good education for your kids, a vacation once a year. Not mansions. Not phony paper wealth. But basic stuff. Basic, *attainable* stuff. There was room for everyone to achieve nearly middle class status, but that wasn't good enough. People wanted more, so they bought into the fantasy, the Ponzi scheme. It was a great big bubble and when it burst, everybody suffered. But not equally." He held up a warning finger. "Those still holding on to their bit of hot air, their measure of paper wealth, clung with all their might." He took a breath, then changed tacks. "Okay. Let's get back to economics. We've covered the three Bs: bubbles, busts, and bailouts. Now I want you to go back to the last century, before the three Bs, and talk to me about the structural economic differences between then and now. How about somebody new? Trina?" He looked at the one unscored girl who never said a word. "Anything, Trina?"

Trina's mouth fell open, and she took a few visible breaths. "Yeah, it **was** different," she said.

Mr. Carol leaned forward, waiting for more, but Trina was empty.

"Was it really so different?" Priscilla asked.

· "I'm talking turn of the century," Mr. Carol said. "I'm talking 2000 and before."

"Yeah, I know," Priscilla said. "But it's not as if *everyone* was middle class, right? I mean, there were poor people and rich people, weren't there?"

Mr. Carol nodded. "That's true. So, has *anything* changed between now and then?"

"Of course," Rachel said. "We have the score."

"Let's leave the score out of it for now," Mr. Carol said. "We'll come back to it, but I want to focus on economics here. What happened when the middle class collapsed?"

"Standard of living declined," Clarissa said. "Poverty rates increased."

"Yes," Mr. Carol said. "What else?"

Imani could tell that he was angling for something. He kept glancing at Diego. But Mr. Carol's star student was distracted, staring into the center of the circle of desks. Occasionally, Diego's eye would flick up to Imani. Imani would catch these moments out of the corner of her eye and turn her body farther away from him.

"Okay, guys," Mr. Carol prodded. "What happens to a society that loses its upward mobility?"

"It stagnates?" Logan offered.

"Does it?" Mr. Carol pressed.

Imani was only half listening. Her focus alternated between Diego's roaming eye and her conversation with Ms. Wheeler. A part of her felt guilty for ratting out Diego and his Chaos Foundation, while the other part reveled in the possibility of a sudden score boost.

"Come on, guys," Mr. Carol said.

Imani could no longer take his whining or the denseness of

her fellow students. "It doesn't stagnate," she said. "It becomes unstable."

"Very good," Mr. Carol said. "And why is that?"

Imani had written a paper on the subject the previous semester, putting herself in the shoes of her grandparents, who had endured such rapid reversals of fortune. "Well, you had falling wages, rising unemployment, bankruptcies, strained government services, crumbling infrastructure."

"And contrasted with all of this?" Mr. Carol asked.

"A major concentration of wealth," Imani said. "The New Golden Age." It had been the title of her paper. Mr. Carol had given her an A, and had written practically a dissertation on the backs of all the pages. When he'd run out of space, he'd emailed her the rest of his comments.

"Okay, Rachel," Mr. Carol said. "Now talk to me about what happens next and why."

"What do you mean?" Rachel said, looking panicked.

While Mr. Carol prodded Rachel, Imani went back to glancing at Diego, whom she noticed was still glancing at her.

"Your earlier comment about the score," Mr. Carol said to Rachel. "What's the relation between it and what Imani has just described?"

Rachel tapped her pen against her teeth.

Frustrated, Mr. Carol turned to Priscilla, but Priscilla only shrugged.

"Logan?" Mr. Carol pressed.

"Don't know," he said.

"I'm looking for causal links, folks," Mr. Carol said.

Imani tried to stay focused on what Mr. Carol was saying, but Diego worried her now. Did he know she turned him in to Ms. Wheeler and her mysterious "we"? Was he trying to intimidate her with these furtive glances?

"Come on, folks. I'm trying to get you to connect the dots here. Imani? Diego?"

Diego fidgeted in his chair as if suddenly waking up, but, uncharacteristically, he had nothing to say.

"It created the conditions for the score," Imani said.

"Thank you," Mr. Carol said. "How?"

"Because the American dream was dead," she said. "There was no upward mobility anymore. The division between rich and poor had hardened. Society had become almost like..." She searched for the right word.

"Like a banana republic?" Diego ventured.

Though she couldn't entirely disagree, it irritated Imani to have her sentence finished, especially by him. "I was going to say like a caste system."

"Right," Diego said. "Then Score Corp comes along and claims to restore upward mobility."

"Excuse me," Logan said. "It doesn't just *claim* to restore upward mobility. It actually *does* restore upward mobility."

"For some," Rachel said.

"For the worthy," Logan added.

Rachel threw her head back in laughter.

"No, he's right," Diego said. "The score basically restores the American dream by giving people the opportunity to ascend."

"Excuse me?" Rachel said.

"It's true," Diego said. "No matter who you are or where you come from, you have the same chances with the score as anybody else. Fitness has nothing to do with money. Look at Chiara Hislop and Alejandro Vidal. They weren't born rich, but they're going to end up that way."

Imani's mouth dropped open. Not only was Diego, a rich kid, speaking openly and without embarrassment about money, but he had taken her idea and was making an eloquent case out of it.

Mr. Carol beamed. "I see somebody's been working on his final essay. Nice angle, Diego."

"I'm sorry," Imani said. "Is Diego actually arguing that the score is an *antidote* to the caste system?"

"Yes, Diego is," Diego said.

Imani kept her eyes on Mr. Carol. "Well, he's completely wrong. The score merely replaces one caste system with another."

Mr. Carol grew excited. "How so?" he asked. Imani knew that nothing thrilled him more than to see two students carving each other up, *on topic.*

"Well, I don't know how Diego defines a caste system," Imani said, "but I think when you divide people up into score gangs and prevent all contact between them, you're basically dealing with a caste system."

"It's not a caste system," Diego said. "It's a meritocracy . . . with borders."

Logan laughed. "I like that. No, seriously. For once, Landis is right."

"Semantics," Imani said. "It's a caste system."

"It's a meritocracy," Diego said. "If you work hard and live according to the rules of fitness, you can ascend. If you don't, you have only yourself to blame."

"Yup," Logan said.

"The score empowers people to change," Diego said. He looked right at Imani as he threw her words back at her. "That's the whole philosophy behind the score," he continued. "A more perfect humanity through technology, which, it turns out, is not about mind control and world domination. It's actually about fairness."

The bell put a period at the end of Diego's sentence, preventing Imani's rebuttal. As everyone filed out, Mr. Carol congratulated Imani and Diego on their embrace of the opposing points of view.

"That right there is the height of intellectual maturity," he said to his retreating students. "And I'd like to see more of it in this class. I *expect* to see more of it in your final papers. Okay?"

His students kept walking.

"I know you can hear me!" he said.

Imani and Diego were the last out of the room.

"They heard you," Imani said.

Mr. Carol grabbed his coffee mug and flopped behind his desk. "It won't make a dime's worth of difference." He put his feet up, uncurled his beat-up scroll, and got lost in the Internet.

As Diego passed Imani, he said: *"Meritocracy."*

"Caste system," she said to his retreating back.

"It's both," Mr. Carol said. "Run with it."

"You think?" Imani asked.

He nodded over the rim of his mug. "The Otis people will love it."

During study period, Imani went to the school library, grabbed a tablet, and began searching. History was filled with caste systems, from the complex Hindu and Indian systems to the two-tier ancient Japanese system of samurai versus everyone else.

After half an hour, Imani was sure she had a topic for her Otis essay. She'd never thought of score gangs as a caste system before, but her argument with Diego in class had convinced her that she was on to something. Critiquing the score from a global historical context would lend the essay depth and substance.

Trolling through stories of the Korean *baekjeong* or the kahunas of Hawaii, Imani saw that humans had been mistreating each other in the same ways for thousands of years. And they weren't secretive about it either. They left lots of evidence. From the globe-spanning malfeasance of the slave trade to the petty and disgusting antics of college fraternities, the practitioners of caste-based cruelty acted as if they were proud of it. That people didn't learn from such carefully documented crimes must have driven history teachers mad on a daily basis, Imani thought. It certainly went a long way toward explaining Mr. Carol.

Imani's favorite article was about the untouchables, who

were the lowbies of India's caste system, the difference being that they were born into it and there was no way out. One of the ways people justified such caste systems was by asserting a hierarchy of morals. Those on the top were deemed to be of higher moral character than those on the bottom, but it was always the people on top doing the deeming.

Imani saw the pattern in colonial America, as a way of justifying slavery, which was also a two-tier caste system. Africans were judged to be of low moral character and, therefore, unworthy of the same rights and privileges as whites. By going into service for white society, these lowbies could redeem their low moral standing. As with the untouchables, there was no way out. Even emancipated slaves were lower than white citizens, or to put it in her father's terms, "the man" kept keeping them down.

Once she'd begun looking, Imani found the pattern cropping up everywhere. There were, she knew, many parts of the world where women were still treated as the inferiors of men, with rights and privileges commensurate with their status. And again, there was no way out. In the war-torn wilds of Afghanistan or the kingdom of Saudi Arabia, you couldn't work your way up from female to male.

But these examples presented a problem for Imani because they cast the score in a positive light. After all, as Diego had argued, at least with the score, you could work your way up. As much as she hated to agree with him, she was beginning to see that the score *was* a meritocracy with borders.

Imani was staring at her tablet, trying to nudge the evidence into an argument she could use, when she noticed Amber standing a few feet away.

"Can I talk to you?" Amber whispered.

Imani glanced around the library, where other students worked silently. Amber motioned for Imani to follow her, then led her out of the library and into the nearest girls' bathroom.

Amber checked under the stall doors to make sure no one was listening, then leaned against one of the sinks. "Okay," she said. "I was going to talk to Connor about this, but he's been acting weird lately and I really don't want to make a big mess of this, so I thought I'd come to you first."

Imani disliked Amber. Her rapport issues were of the kind that induced revulsion rather than sympathy, the way Deon's did. But something about the way Amber bit her lip just then made her seem vulnerable.

"I think we should boot Deon," Amber said.

"What? Why? We don't even get our scores for another week." Imani went straight back to disliking Amber.

"Yeah, Imani, but dumping him when he's already dropped out of the sixties is just *expected*. I mean, do we get any score boost from that at all?"

"What makes you think he's dropping out of the sixties?"

Amber shook her head. "Are you blind or something? He's practically retarded, you know."

The statement was untrue, offensive, and wrong in so many ways, Imani didn't know where to begin. "I like Deon," she said calmly.

"So you're just, like, giving up on your peer group issues

completely? I thought when you dropped Cady Fazio you were serious about changing. I was hoping you'd be an ally in this."

Now Imani understood. Amber was operating under the assumption that Imani would rise now that she'd dropped Cady, and that by forging a bond with Imani through this action against Deon, Amber would benefit by association. It was fairly standard, as gamesmanship went.

"Oh, forget it," Amber said. "I can organize this without you." She faced the mirror and wiped away a mascara smudge beneath her left eye. "Jayla's already said she wants to dump him. I only need a few others. Just don't say anything to Deon, okay? Or Connor. This is my thing, not his."

As Amber fluffed her unruly curls, Imani couldn't help but think about the other things they had in common: freckles over the nose, a sense of panic about their final scores, and a keen sense of the tick of the clock.

"Okay, Imani?" Amber pressed.

"Don't worry," Imani said. "I'm sure you'll get full credit."

When Imani got home that day, she went straight upstairs, sat on her bed, and spread out the articles she'd printed at the school library. She was hoping for a flash of brilliance, but her research wouldn't cooperate. Every comparison between the score and the human race's other attempts to divide each other into groups flattered the score.

Outside her window, she could see her father's legs sticking out from underneath the Madsens' sport fisherman. Imani paused to watch her mother, bundled into a giant wool sweater, squat next to her father, a mug of cocoa in one hand and a wrench in the other. It wasn't necessary for her mother to be there. Her father could get his own tools. But Imani knew there was nothing else for her to do. When things were slow for her father, he'd hang out with her mother in the bait shop reading catalogs and complaining about the price of everything.

Camaraderie. That was what they had. Life was tough at LeMonde Marina. Though her mother did her best to shield Imani and her brother from the truth, Imani knew they were barely making ends meet. But her mother and father were in it together. That fact might not have changed the numbers in their bank account, but it made the situation a lot less depressing. There was a kind of nobility to it. Theirs was a challenge to be overcome, an opportunity for triumph, resilience, and other fine things.

When Imani glanced down at an article on American slaves, she realized that the slaves too had camaraderie, some of them anyway. They sang songs in the fields and wrote slave narratives describing their lives. By working together with like-minded people, they formed the Underground Railroad. Later, their descendants, who were still the lowbies of American society, forged the civil rights movement.

After rereading that article, she dug out another one, on an organization of Saudi women who were fighting for emancipation. Camaraderie again. These women risked their lives to work for freedom, not merely for themselves but for all Saudi women.

In both of those cases, the lowbies of society worked

together to fight the caste system itself. But the scored never did that. Whenever they fought, it was always against each other. Like Amber and her dirty scheme to dump Deon, the scored plotted and backstabbed in an effort to ascend. *Because they believed they could.*

That was the difference, Imani thought.

The American slaves *couldn't* ascend. There was no possibility of working your way up from black to white. The same was true for those women in Saudi Arabia. No matter how hard you worked, a woman could never become a man. Slavery and sexism were not merit-based caste systems. You couldn't work the system, so the lowbies had no choice but to take the system down.

Finally, Imani's research was working for her. As she stared out the window to where her mother slid a set of pliers to her father, still wedged under the Madsens' boat, she couldn't suppress a victorious chuckle.

15. sherry potter

ON TUESDAY, MR. Carol gave in to the curriculum Nazis. After a brief resumption of his discussion of the collapse of the middle class, he abruptly turned his attention to the material he was "under contract to cover." Namely, the Great Recovery, which he didn't believe in but which Imani and her fellow students would be tested on at the end of the year.

Everything he said was downloadable from the Massachusetts curriculum website, so there was little point in paying attention, and Mr. Carol went at the material like a bored carnival barker hawking the same lousy stuffed animals. Imani took notes, just to keep her mind—and her eyes—off of Diego, who she could tell was stealing glances at her again. She wished he'd stop.

After class, Diego followed her into the hallway. When a

cluster of freshmen blocked her way, Imani stopped suddenly, and Diego walked right into her, his chin grazing the back of her head.

"So sorry," he whispered. He slid his cool hand down her arm, pressed the folded paper into her hand, and whisked away in a rush of air that smelled of honeysuckle and something else Imani couldn't place. There was an eyeball directly overhead, and it intrigued Imani that Diego believed he had fooled it. Perhaps he had. But once he was out of sight, she opened the note right in front of the eyeball. She had nothing to hide, after all. This was part of her mission to extract information on behalf of the score.

You're in good company with your theory about gangs as a caste system. Sherry Potter herself agreed with you. I've been digging around my mom's files, and I may have some useful things for you. If you want to look through them, come to my house tonight. No eyeballs, and you can get there by boat. Just be careful on the cliff steps. I'm at 3 Corona Point Road.

Diego L., Overblown Twit

Imani's peers rushed past her as she read and reread the address, the letters towering like the location they described. In all likelihood, Diego was a millionaire's son. Perhaps, she thought, that was the source of his outsized self-confidence. He was the only Corona Point resident at Somerton High, which meant that he was, by a wide margin, the richest kid in school.

But all the money in the world didn't change the fact that he had just unknowingly invited a spy to peer into his mother's files. Ms. Wheeler, Imani thought, would rejoice.

That night, Imani told her parents she was meeting her gang again at the library. To keep up the ruse, she rode her bike halfway down Marina Road, tucked it into the marsh reeds, and snuck back to the marina. She paddled Frankenwhaler far enough down the river to be sure they wouldn't hear, then started her up and sped for Corona Point.

The tide was coming in, but it was still low enough to make the river a minefield of dangerous shallows. With the muddy banks looming even higher, forty miles per hour felt like sixty. Her father would have killed her for taking the curves so steeply, but Imani couldn't resist. There was no traffic to interfere with the sweet hum of her motor, no other wakes to interrupt her own. The air felt cleaner when there was no one else breathing it and Imani could imagine that the river was fertile again.

Speeding up at Goodwell's Fish House, where the river made an S, Imani reveled in the deep turns that brought her so close to the mud flats she could smell the rot. As the lights of Somerton faded from view, she aimed for Corona Point, the frigid air lashing her face. Once into the rough waters of the channel, she searched for markers of the old marina. Only a few rotting pylons and some warped dock fragments remained. With help from the sliver of moon, Imani steered around them, then cut the motor and drifted onto the fringe of beach.

After pulling the boat onto the sand, she trekked through low bushes and reeds until she found the steps that led up the cliffs. The steps had been built when the land was publicly owned, but after years of neglect, they were loose, overgrown with weeds, and, in some cases, missing. It was a treacherous climb, but if the bottles littered about were any indication, the off-limits signs were being ignored.

When Imani made it to the top, she found herself in someone's giant backyard. It took a few minutes to get to the front of the house, then another five minutes down a long woodsy driveway to Corona Point Road. There she found a wooden sign with WHIMSY written on it. Imani rolled her eyes and thought of her dad, who had once joked that the people of Corona Point gave their homes names because numbers weren't good enough for them.

Imani set off down the road beneath the dark canopy of trees, passing "Cliff Haven," "Moonrise," and the ludicrously understated "Mooney Hut." Eventually, she found some driveways with actual numbers on them and was able to follow them to number three, a house with no name. Its driveway was unpaved, and the trees and bushes on either side were overgrown. The driveway brought Imani to a stone mansion, three stories high. It was one of the older homes, smaller than the others, better integrated into its natural environment, but still basically a castle. The house was dark except for two rooms— one on the first floor and one on the third.

Imani walked around the side just to see what was there. She found a covered swimming pool, a trampoline, a stone

barbecue, a wrought iron table with matching chairs, and a cro-
quet game that had stopped mid-play. Underneath a gigantic
deck was Diego's black scooter. Imani heard nothing at first,
but as she returned to the front of the house, she noticed the
tinkling of piano playing. At the stone walkway that led to the
front door, a motion-triggered light came on.

The piano music stopped. Imani froze and had a quick
debate with herself over staying versus fleeing, which was interrupted by the front door opening. She took a deep breath and
tried to appear unintimidated by her surroundings.

"You showed up," Diego said. He was barefoot, wearing
jeans and a white T-shirt. "Did you take the cliff steps?"

"Yes," Imani said. "And I almost died three times. I should
sue you."

"Good luck," Diego said, grinning. "My mother's a lawyer."

"So I've heard," she said.

He held the door open and she went in.

The interior of the house was crisply modern, with
heavy, dark wooden furniture and large unframed paintings
on the walls. In his cavernous kitchen, outfitted with gleaming
professional grade appliances, Diego offered Imani a soda,
which she declined with a shake of the head. He led her
through an even more gargantuan living room, with floor-to-
ceiling bookshelves on two walls and a grand piano in the center of it. Piano music was spread out on the stand, the bench,
and the floor.

"My parents are out," Diego said. "But I dragged some of
my mom's boxes into my room."

He didn't wait for Imani to say anything, and, after a moment's hesitation, she followed him up a wide spiral staircase, edged with stacks of books.

"You guys read a lot, huh?" she asked.

"That's my dad. My mom put a moratorium on bookshelves to try to stop him, so now he just leaves them around the house."

They skipped the second floor, where, Diego explained, his "pack rat" father kept the rest of his books, going straight up to the third.

In keeping with the scale of the house, Diego's room was more of an apartment than a bedroom. Not only did he have his own bathroom, he had his own *kitchen*.

"Wow," Imani said. "Do you have to pay rent?"

He laughed politely, then pointed to the foot of his bed, where three cardboard boxes interrupted the pattern of a Persian rug. He had sheet music framed on the walls.

"My mom doesn't know I took these, so we have to make sure everything goes back in order." Diego sat cross-legged in front of the boxes. "If we can figure out the order. I don't think it's alphabetical."

Imani sat opposite him, noting the tight weave and subtle sheen of the rug. The LeMondes had a "Persian" rug in their living room too. It was from Kmart, and you could see the digitized edges of the design screen-printed onto it.

"You know my mother's semi-famous, right?" Diego asked.

Imani shrugged. Her own mother was not semi-famous, although she did win a clam chowder contest once and got to meet one of the Red Sox players. In the news coverage, you could sort of see her in the background, behind the reporter and the Red Sox player.

"You should interview her," he said. "People are always doing that. She's incredibly busy, but I think she'd find the time. But if you ask dumb questions, she'll walk out. She does that."

"I wouldn't ask dumb questions."

"She'd probably make allowances for your age anyway." He grabbed a stack of papers that were stapled together and sitting on top of one of the boxes. "I thought this might be useful. It's from an interview Sherry Potter gave just a few months before she disappeared." He flipped through the pages until he found the relevant paragraph, then read aloud: " 'The focus on peer group is sound and based on very good data. I'm not denying that. But what we've done, I'm afraid, is to create a kind of caste system.' " He paused to look up at Imani meaningfully. " 'And it's been . . . well, shocking, to put it mildly, to see how obediently kids have organized themselves into it. You have to understand that was *never our intent.*' " He pointed out those final three words to Imani, then handed her the stack of pages. "Useful?" he asked.

Imani flipped to the front page. The interview was from *Neuroscience Quarterly* and went on for about twenty pages. "Potentially," Imani said.

"Some people think score gangs are the reason Sherry Potter bugged out and went underground," Diego said. "Later on, she compares the whole system to *Brave New World*. But you probably haven't read that, have you?"

She hadn't. "Don't tell me." She sighed with faux boredom. "It used to be required reading?"

"Ask your parents."

"Whatever." Imani started skimming the interview. It did seem to be full of evidence in support of her thesis that the score created a type of caste system. "That's strange," she said. "I don't see the phrase 'meritocracy with borders' anywhere." She shook the pages as if the phrase might fall out.

"Semantics," Diego said with a dismissive wave. "The important thing is the *type* of caste system it is, which is why for *my* essay I'm going to compare the score to other caste systems."

Imani looked at him in horror. "But that's *my* idea."

"I figured," he said. "I'm taking the opposite position." He grinned at her. "You want to hear my thesis?"

Imani fumed silently for a few seconds, then pretended not to care. "Can I stop you from telling me?"

"Don't try to be funny."

Imani felt her anger rising. "Don't try to be superior."

"Okay," he laughed. "Anyway, what I'm going to argue is that—"

"Because you're *not* superior to me," Imani broke in, anger getting the better of her. She took a breath and softened her tone. "Regardless of what you may think."

"How do you know what I think?" Diego's blue eye zeroed in on her.

Imani held his gaze, determined to prove that she was not intimidated, either by his attitude or his wealth. They didn't move, they didn't even blink, until a single drip from the faucet broke the standoff. When Imani looked away, Diego marked her defeat with a chuckle. "Please continue," he said. "You were about to prove my point."

She surveyed his kitchen to avoid looking at him. "Was I?" she asked.

"Brilliantly too."

"Oh, please enlighten me."

"Fine," Diego said. "I'm going to argue that human beings have a natural tendency to rank themselves."

"So?" Imani scoffed.

"*So.*" He mimicked her tone. "We can say all we want about equality, but we don't believe in it. We believe in superiority and inferiority. It's in our nature to rank ourselves into status groups."

"Exactly," Imani said. "Like score gangs."

"Yes, but even before the score, there were gangs. There were jocks and geeks. There were popular kids and misfits. There were greasers and squares."

"Rich and poor."

Diego paused for a moment to absorb her comment, but he didn't rise to it. "Exactly," he said. "It's in our nature."

"And we're still doing it," she reminded him. "Only now it's scientific."

"No," Diego said. "That's where you're wrong. Score gangs are a bug, not a feature. If used properly, the score can be a pattern interrupt that breaks groups down."

Pattern interrupt. Was this another phrase from that interview with the Potter-Kleins? she wondered. Had she fed him this line of inquiry herself? Diego grabbed the interview from her and flipped through the pages in search of something. "Here." He read aloud. "'The score was meant to empower the individual, but instead the opposite has happened. Score gangs have become a crutch, a way for kids to *avoid* making conscious decisions about their peer group. As such, they've become, at best, first element neutral. At worst, they actually limit mobility.'"

"Wait," she said. "So you're saying—"

"I'm not saying it. Sherry Potter is."

Imani read the section herself. According to Sherry Potter, you didn't have to sit with the 60s just because you were a 60. The software didn't care where you ate lunch. The gangs were never part of the Potter-Kleins' original intent. "I don't believe it," she said.

"Neither did I at first."

Imani hated gangs. They were the reason she'd made that pact with Cady. She couldn't tolerate the idea that everyone she cared about could disappear from her life overnight. But she'd always assumed gangs were a necessary part of scored life. What if they weren't?

"So." Diego leaned back against the edge of his bed. "Thoughts? Comments? Am I missing something?"

Imani labored to find fault with his case. Though she considered it original and potentially groundbreaking, she couldn't bear to see him looking so smug. By rights, he should have been wrong. Demonstrably and, if at all possible, *laughably* wrong. "It's good," she conceded.

"Thank you." Diego bowed.

"But," she said.

"There's a but?"

Imani's mind swirled.

"No way," he said. "This baby is rock solid. Everything bad about the score is the result of its misuse."

"You don't really believe that," she said.

"For the purposes of this paper, I do."

Imani could see Diego's competitive streak coming out, and she was only too happy to take her shot. "Fine," she said. "I can agree that the score—if used properly—empowers the individual over the group. But you're assuming that groups are inherently bad, which, of course, they're not."

"Yes, they are," he said. "As soon as you have groups, the individual is suppressed."

"Sometimes the individual *needs* to be suppressed."

"Okay," he said. "You need to know that you really frighten me sometimes."

Imani laughed. "Your worldview is so narrow. You're not thinking globally. You're not thinking historically."

Diego stared at her blankly.

"Let's take the caste system of gender," she said. "Take Saudi Arabia."

"No thanks," he said.

"Don't try to be funny," she said. "Anyway, how do you think women's emancipation will be achieved there, if it ever is? Will each of them achieve it separately? As individuals?"

"Well, no."

"Exactly. They have to work together. But what do you

think would happen if gender were the kind of caste system that empowered the individual?"

"What do you mean?"

"What if it were possible to work your way up from female to male?"

Diego inclined his head. "That's absurd."

"It's called a thought experiment. If it *were* possible, do you think women would band together to fight for their freedom? Or would they beat each other down in an effort to rise up?"

Diego's expression darkened.

"What I'm saying is that you're right," Imani continued. "The score does empower the individual over the group. Your closest friend today might be invisible to you tomorrow. It doesn't matter how long you've been friends or how much you care about each other, you have to be willing to sacrifice anyone to get ahead. The only allegiance you're rewarded for is allegiance to the score. Anil Hanesh knew that. We used to be friends. And now I don't exist to him. That's how he became a high ninety. That's how the score elevates the individual above the group."

Diego shook his head vigorously. "That's not what I'm arguing."

"Well, you can pretty it up any way you want," Imani said. "The fact of the matter is that the score prevents long-term bonding between individuals by empowering them as individuals. Whereas with other caste systems, like slavery and female oppression, the individual is disempowered. And because there's no way for the individual to work the system, they're able to find common cause."

"I bet there were slaves who worked the system."

"They didn't become white, though, did they?"

The rhythm of their debate came to a halt as Diego fidgeted in discomfort, the way white people sometimes did when people of color brought up race. It was as if he presumed Imani was incorporating him into the general guilt pool for historical transgressions. She wasn't, and she resented having her dominance of the debate sidetracked by such a generic display of white guilt.

Diego recovered quickly enough, though. "Wait. So you're saying that slavery and female oppression are *better* than the score because they disempower the individual?"

"What I'm saying is that those caste systems can *fall* because they disempower the individual. Call it a bug, not a feature, if you want. But it's *why* they can fall. And it's why the score, unlike those other caste systems, will probably last forever."

There was a brief pause, then Diego's mouth fell open. He wanted to disagree. Imani could see that. He was looking for some essential point she had overlooked. After a pause that seemed to drain the life from him, he stood up and went to his kitchen. He opened the small refrigerator and took out two bottles of beer. Imani stared in disbelief. Who kept beer in their bedroom? He opened them both with a bottle opener, had a sip from one, and pushed the other across the counter.

"Uh, I don't drink," she said.

He had another sip, then stared across the counter, not at her, and not through her, but rather as if she weren't there anymore. A lesser version of herself would have derived some pleasure from the fact that she had driven Diego to drink with the sheer force of her argument. But what Imani really wanted was for him to disagree. Dissent was the background noise of their relationship. And, she realized now, something she actually enjoyed.

"Hey, you know what we should do?" he asked, the pall of his expression brightening suddenly.

Fight, she thought. *Argue. Compete.*

"We should write one paper," he said. "Together. We could begin with my idea, laying out the case for individualism through the score. Then we could show how, in a totally disgusting irony, it ends up crushing the individual in the end."

"Cheery," she said.

"It would get their attention. Especially if they knew it was a collaboration between a scored and an unscored."

It wasn't a terrible idea, she thought. From the tense equilibrium of their sparring, strange and original ideas had already evolved. "But what about the money?" she asked.

"You could have it," he said. "I don't need it."

Imani's eyes wandered across the row of professional-grade appliances behind him, all with long European names. Of course he didn't need the scholarship. A yard sale of the contents of that room could pay for a semester's tuition.

"So why do you care so much about this essay?" she asked. "I thought you wanted to win."

"I do."

"Why?"

"To prove I can."

Imani stared at him, dumbfounded, then stood up and went to the window, which overlooked the swimming pool. What an infuriating answer, she thought. The Otis Scholarship was a lifeline for her, and Diego was treating it like a Boy Scout badge. "Do you know what I'm risking to be here?" she asked. She kept her back to him.

"I figured you'd calculated the risks," he said. "Look, if I win, I'll give you the money. I was planning to do that from the beginning."

Imani turned from the window and faced him. "I would never take money from you," she said. "Do you understand that? Never."

Diego held his hands out in front of him. "Okay, okay. Fine. I'm sorry." He grabbed both beers and held one out for her.

"I told you I don't drink."

He sidled around the counter and walked toward her. "It's not score negative," he said. "I looked it up."

Imani sighed in frustration. "Its effects are almost *always* score negative," she said.

Diego shook his head. "Alcohol can be consumed in an environment of fitness as long as it's done in moderation and without the intent to induce intoxication." He stopped a few feet away from her. "I read that."

"Given that I don't drink *at all*," she said, "intoxication is inevitable."

Diego stood his ground, grinning his predatory grin. "Write the essay with me," he said.

"No."

"We'll nail it," he said. "My mother might even be able to get it published somewhere. She's got connections. So does my dad, for that matter. He teaches political science at St. James."

"I don't want your family connections," she said. "I don't want your beer, and I don't want your fucking charity!"

Diego blinked rapidly, and Imani turned away and looked out the window again. Leaves had accumulated in the valleys between air bubbles on the pool cover. Imani wondered whose job it was to clear them out. Probably some parent of a Somerton High student, she figured.

For a long time, they both stood silently while the faucet continued its slow, intermittent drip. Then Imani heard Diego place the two bottles of beer on a coffee table.

"Why do you need to hate me so much?" he asked quietly.

She kept her back to him. "I don't *need* anything from you."

Beyond the swimming pool and the broad expanse of lawn was the cliff. Imani tried to remember where the cliff steps were in relation to Diego's house. Was there a shortcut? A way back that would not take her past Whimsy and the other named castles?

"Imani?"

She wouldn't face him. She felt uncomfortable just being there.

"I hope you win," he said. "Whether it's with me or against

me. I'm not saying I won't try to beat you. But I hope you win. I hope you get everything you want in life."

The window was dark enough to produce a crisp reflection of him, but Imani couldn't read his expression, so she assumed he was mocking her.

"Thanks," she said.

Then she contemplated the cliff steps, which would be even more dangerous on the descent.

16. gum wrappers

IT HAD BEEN warm that Tuesday afternoon, the kind of day May promised but rarely delivered. While Imani had been in her bedroom doing homework before her visit to Diego's house, Cady and Parker had gone to the Taylors' farm field. There were no eyeballs present. They went there to be alone. A maple tree shaded them from the sun, and the nearest road was obscured behind some gently rolling hills. But there had been nothing between them and a pair of sophomore 40s lying belly-down in some corn. They weren't close enough to record sound, but their telephoto lens was sharp and their camera work, if not exactly professional, was steady and focused.

By the time Cady and Parker were pulling their pants back on, the footage was already uploaded. By the time they left the farm field, it had been tagged, rated, and ranked. It went viral overnight.

By Wednesday morning, those who weren't describing the footage in detail were listening to those details. All tablets in the school library were occupied. Still images were slapped up in the boys' rooms and scattered on the hallway floors.

It wasn't the first time a pair of Somerton High students had disgraced themselves online. Amateur porn was the lifeblood of the Internet, and always had been. But this was different. "Farm Field Follies," a.k.a. "Farm Field F*&k Fest," was a cautionary tale about a former 90 throwing it all away to have sex with an unscored in public. The fact that Cady had already been a 70 when she'd begun dating Parker wasn't discussed, nor was the fact that they had never intended for their act to be public. Minus these complicating details, Cady's descent was like the story of Chiara Hislop in reverse. Such stories were the narrative backbone of the score.

At lunch that day, Imani's gang kept staring at her, as if she were involved somehow, or at least mildly contaminated by the incident. Imani ignored them. She had nothing to say on the topic that hadn't already been said a hundred times, and she wasn't the least bit interested in her gang's analysis of it. She'd heard about it herself in homeroom, but had refused to look at the footage out of respect for Cady.

"So?" Connor said eventually. "Did you hear, or what?"

Imani looked at him as if he were an idiot. It was impossible *not* to have heard. At that very moment, some junior lowbies at a nearby table were reenacting a portion of the footage. Hastily printed still images were scattered all over the lunchroom floor. Then it occurred to Imani that Connor might have been speaking of something new. Was it possible that Cady had found the time to engage in *another* scandalous act?

"Heard what?" she asked, dreading the answer.

Amber couldn't wait. "Ms. Wheeler was waiting for them at the back entrance. She told them to turn around and go right back home. Ex*pelled*!"

"She can't expel them," Imani said.

"Oh my God," Amber said. "Have you *seen* that video?"

"No. Have you?"

"I . . . no, but . . . somebody described it to me."

"Well, then you know it didn't take place on school property," Imani said.

"So?" Amber said.

"So you can't expel someone for having sex in a farm field."

"There was the graffiti too," Amber said. "Don't forget about that."

"There's no proof they did that," Imani said.

"I thought there were witnesses," Jayla said.

"Yeah," Imani said. "The same jerks who spied on them in that farm field. The same *forties*, incidentally, who filmed them, then uploaded the footage for everyone to see."

"Why are you defending them?" Connor asked, his eyes flicking to the eyeball above Imani's head.

"Well gamed, Connor," Imani said. "But I think the software

is smart enough to know the difference between defending an unfit act and defending someone's right to an education. You can't expel someone for having sex. It's probably not even legal. Deon, what are you doing?"

Deon had reached for something under the table, and now his large brown eyes bulged. When Jayla leaned across the table to have a look, her hands folded protectively over her face.

"Deon, you should put that down," Jayla said.

But Deon could not tear his eyes away. Eventually, Connor grabbed the paper from Deon's hands, looked at the image with clinical coolness, then turned it facedown on the table.

There it sat, white and square, its image shielded from view. No one said a word, and no one looked away. But while the others merely stared at it, grimly committed to leaving it facedown (though wanting to turn it over), Deon seemed transformed by it. No one was more sheltered than Deon; no one had less intimacy with his fellow human beings. Now he had glimpsed the ultimate intimacy.

"I have to go," Imani said. She got up and tossed the rest of her sandwich on the way to the exit.

Ms. Wheeler was surprised to see Imani, but she invited her into her office. "I take it you've heard about Cady," she said. "Shut the door and sit down."

Imani closed the door but remained standing. "I don't understand how you can expel them," she said, struggling to restrain her anger. "Is that even legal?"

"Things aren't always so black-and-white, Imani." Ms. Wheeler maintained her pleasant demeanor, but Imani could tell she was insulted by the question. "Sometimes the best strategy is to throw something at the wall and see if it sticks." She paused. "Aren't you going to sit?"

Imani shook her head.

"You're upset," she said. "You still care about Cady. You realize, of course, that's not going to help your score."

"I just don't understand how you can expel them for something they did in private."

"The lawyers will work all of that out." Ms. Wheeler flicked her hand as if at a bloom of flies. "They're both being represented by Dena Landis."

"They are?"

Ms. Wheeler nodded, a glimmer of self-satisfied joy on her face. "We've had to schedule an emergency meeting for tomorrow night. Parents, teachers, lawyers, press. They'll all be there."

"Press?" Imani asked.

"Dena Landis rarely appears without a phalanx of journalists." Ms. Wheeler rolled her eyes. "I'm not worried. Actually, I'm hoping to have something on her son in time for the meeting." Her lips curled into a smile. "Thanks to you. The press will eat that up, don't you think? Dena Landis's own son arrested."

"Arrested?" Imani pulled out a chair and sat down. "For what? You're not talking about the Chaos Foundation meeting tonight, are you? Don't they have to be committing a crime first? Isn't there a right to free assembly?"

"Well, aren't you an informed citizen," Ms. Wheeler said, arching an eyebrow. "I suppose you've learned these phrases in Mr. Carol's class."

Imani had, but that seemed beside the point.

"Anyway," Ms. Wheeler said, "I think you've forgotten about the incident at Chauncey Beach?"

"You mean the fire in the dunes?" she said. "But what does that have to do with anything?"

"You said yourself they were trying to draw out the authorities."

"That was just a guess!"

Ms. Wheeler held up her palms. "Look. Who knows what they were doing back there? The point is that these people think they're above the law. And we're going to demonstrate that they're not." She leaned back in her leather chair. "You're not worried about Diego Landis, are you? Has he gotten to you?"

Imani wasn't sure what Ms. Wheeler meant by that, but she knew she didn't want to be responsible for Diego's *arrest*. That was never part of the deal.

"Well, I wouldn't worry about him anyway," Ms. Wheeler said. "At best, he'll spend a day or two in jail. This is just for show. But it'll keep Dena Landis occupied for a while. You see, we're usually on the back foot with these people. They act. We react. We never know what they're going to throw at us, so we're never prepared. It's a smart strategy, so I've borrowed it. I'm going to throw everything at them at once. An expulsion, an arrest, and an emergency town referendum to ban all unscored from Somerton High." Ms. Wheeler's eyes seemed to glow with the idea.

Imani was speechless. She'd never seen Ms. Wheeler like this before.

"I've already gotten the town council's support for it," Ms. Wheeler continued. "They're in total agreement that something has to be done. We can't just stand by idly while the unscored victimize our children. Cady Fazio was a seventy before she met Parker Gray. A *seventy*."

"I know," Imani said flatly.

"She could have worked in retail, health services. At seventy, there are real possibilities. And now look at her." Ms. Wheeler shook her head in pity.

But Imani was unconvinced by the display. Only last week, Ms. Wheeler had congratulated her for "discarding" Cady. Did she now expect Imani to believe that Cady mattered?

"Of course, none of this should concern you," Ms. Wheeler said. "You should be focusing on yourself, and your own fitness. That's the important thing. You'll see. You'll be over that scholarship line before you know it." She flashed Imani her radiant smile, then unfurled her tap pad and began typing.

"But–" Imani cut herself off. She was going to remind Ms. Wheeler that getting over the scholarship line was out of the question, a fact that had necessitated the whole scheme with Diego Landis in the first place. But the ease with which Ms. Wheeler had forgotten those details, which in the past would have made Imani feel small, made her angry. Now that Ms.

Wheeler had gotten what she needed, she was dismissing Imani with generic reassurances. She was treating Imani like a detail to be smoothed over, a gum wrapper to be discarded.

Ms. Wheeler didn't look up when Imani stood and opened the door to leave.

"Close it on the way out, will you?" Ms. Wheeler said.

Imani left the door open. There were still ten minutes left of lunch, but she didn't return to the lunchroom. She went straight to her locker, grabbed her coat and backpack, and left.

Once outside, she ran all the way down the Causeway.

17. the river of unknowing

NEXT TO THE battered mermaid in the Abruzzi Antiques parking lot was a cement swan with only one wing. Imani stared at it while sitting on the stone elephant, her legs swinging back and forth. Where had the Abruzzis found these broken creatures, she wondered, and why? Who would buy them? She couldn't imagine anyone going to the trouble of hauling one into a truck and carrying it away. Maybe the Abruzzis had bought them to keep them company.

It was warm and bright. Imani slid out of her coat and told herself to stand up and face the eyeball. But her body wouldn't move. It preferred keeping her at eye level with the stone creatures. She felt at home with them, as if she were part of that unwanted zoo–so full of promise once, but now terminally damaged.

Imani lay back on the cool cement of the elephant's back. The eyeball dangling above was a black spot against the bright blue sky, inviting her confession. But Imani wasn't sure what her sins were. They seemed to contradict each other. In the end, she knew it wouldn't matter anyway. The software already knew.

The software knew everything.

Imani skipped dinner, claiming a stomachache, and spent the evening in her room doing, and redoing, her Spanish homework. Just after eight o'clock, her father's heavy footsteps climbed the stairs. To avoid having to speak with him, she dug out her Spanish book and started redoing her homework once more.

Her father knocked twice, then opened the door and peeked in. "I brought you some bread," he said. When she didn't respond right away, he opened the door and entered, holding out a buttered slice of toast on a paper towel. "You gotta eat something."

"Thanks." Imani took it from him and nibbled a corner, keeping her Spanish book open meaningfully.

Her father was undeterred. "Isiah says there's a school meeting tomorrow night? Something for parents?" He sat on the edge of her bed, and Imani moved over to make room for him.

"Yeah, but don't bother," she said. "Isn't Isiah's scrimmage tomorrow night?"

"I just want to make sure we're represented, that's all."

Imani laughed gently. It was so typical of her father to believe he would have some say in what transpired with Ms. Wheeler and the town council. Though frequently cynical about the abuses of the rich and powerful, her father was, at heart, an idealist. Imani had always liked this about him.

"They're not voting," she said. "I think there's going to be a referendum vote at some point, but this is just a show meeting. It's basically Ms. Wheeler and the town council trying to convince everyone to ban the unscored from school."

Her father sucked in air through his teeth. "Is this because of what happened with Cady and that video?"

"Uh-huh."

"And now they want to ban *all* the unscored? Can they do that?"

"Maybe," she said. In the end, she knew the lawyers would hash it out according to laws and statutes neither she nor her father would understand. But if Ms. Wheeler got her referendum vote, Imani suspected she'd win at the polls. There were more scored than unscored in Somerton, and they would vote in the interest of their children.

Her father was shaking his head. "It just doesn't seem right to me," he said. "Don't those kids deserve an education, just like anyone else? It doesn't seem right at all."

Imani snorted. What did right and wrong have to do with anything?

Her father sighed in frustration. "So I take it you don't want to discuss this," he said. "Even though it's about your best friend."

There was a tone of judgment that Imani found difficult to take, given how much she had struggled with the choices she'd made and how little he understood that struggle. She closed her Spanish book and put down her pen. "Okay, let's talk about it then. Let's talk about how my *best friend* threw her life *and* my life away so she could date Parker Gray. Let's talk about how we can all be 'represented' by attending some pointless meeting whose only real purpose is for Ms. Wheeler to make Dena Landis look foolish. Let's pretend this is a problem we can solve using old-fashioned common sense and morality, as if these things had any relevance in the world *at all*!"

As Imani spoke, her father's face hardened. "Now you listen here, Imani Jane. You know as well as I do that I *will* not have you speaking to me that way."

"Fine." She opened her Spanish book and resumed conjugating verbs.

"I did not say we were finished."

Imani kept her head in her Spanish book, fully expecting him to pluck it from her hands and throw it onto the floor. When a muscle in his arm tensed she waited for the fallout, but he stayed put, the fire of his temper fading quickly into something closer to sadness. In a voice so soft Imani hardly recognized it, he said: "Where did you go, Imani?"

She would have preferred the fire. When she didn't answer, he sat and stared at his oil-stained fingers. Imani went back to her verbs, screwing up her face in pretend concentration, but all she could sense was her father's large presence and his even larger sadness. He seemed as alone with it, despite their proximity, as she was alone with her own troubles. Between the two of them was a river of unknowing.

After a while, her father stood up, the bed bouncing back lighter than air. His footsteps descended the stairs. Imani could hear him speaking to her mother quietly, but not quietly enough, about how "family don't mean nothing anymore." Her mother tried to comfort him, but even from that distance, Imani could hear the strain in her voice. This was clearly a topic familiar to both of them, though new to Imani. She picked out a few words here and there: "your own children," "opportunity," "lost," and, from her father, "equalize, my ass." When her mother failed to quiet him, she pulled him into the kitchen, where their discussion grew unintelligible.

Imani listened to the rise and fall of their voices for a while, wondering what it was they thought they'd "lost." Then, at 8:17, having had enough of that day, she turned off the light, slipped under the covers, and closed her eyes.

Sleep never came.

18. stone creatures

MARINA ROAD WAS darker than it had ever been. No clouds, no moon, and the sky a dense black whose pinprick stars seemed to hoard their light. Imani crept slowly between the swaying marsh reeds, trying to be soothed by the cool air, but it only energized her fear. And the smell of life and death in multitudes unseen beyond the tall reeds allowed her merely to *pretend* to a sense of perspective on what she was doing. She was one small person of billions, a member of one species of billions. In the long historical scheme of things, her actions were insignificant, her choices minor, her mistakes trifling. But despite all of that, her fear was as big as the sky itself.

When she reached the end of Marina Road, the Causeway was deserted. On either side, widely spaced streetlights cast small pools of light, one of them capturing the stone elephant and the eyeball dangling above it, an eyeball she now thought of as her own.

Imani removed her cell from her pocket and dialed a number she'd wanted to dial for two weeks. After six rings, the familiar voice said: "I'm doing very important things. Leave a message."

There was a beep, then a pause, in which Imani accepted that she was ruining her score for good. "Call me back," she said. "It's an emergency. I mean it."

When she hung up, a car drove by. Imani crouched into the bank of marsh reeds, the impulse to hide her actions having become, by now, an instinct. Her cell buzzed in her palm.

"Why are you calling me?" Cady asked. "What are you doing?"

"I need a favor," Imani said. "I need to call Diego Landis. Do you have his number? Does Parker?"

"What are you talking about?" Cady sounded worried. "Where are you?"

"It's really important that I get in touch with him right now," Imani pleaded. "Doesn't Parker know him? Are you with him now?"

Cady paused before answering. "You're not being very smart."

"Please, Cady."

"I'll call you back," Cady said, then hung up.

It was getting cold. Imani had only grabbed a light coat as she left the house, not wanting to wake her parents.

Her cell buzzed again.

"Parker just called him," Cady said. "He's not answering."

Imani slumped into the cold sand.

"Why are you calling Diego Landis anyway?" Cady asked. "Why are you calling *me*?"

"Cady, I need a ride."

Cady sighed heavily. "What have you done?"

Imani didn't answer right away. Though unable to cast her behavior in a moral framework of any enduring solidity, she knew that what she had done was, in some indefinable way, wrong. So she began at the beginning, with Diego's proposal, then told Cady the whole story. She left nothing out, and when she had finished, it was so quiet she would have sworn she heard Cady breathing. "Are you still there?" Imani asked.

"I can't believe you did that" was the answer. "I really can't believe you—"

There was a click, then a dial tone.

"Cady?" Imani said, her voice shaking.

Cady had hung up.

Imani looked at her cell. It was 9:47. Even if she went back to get her bicycle, she wouldn't have made it to St. James in time to warn Diego. In all likelihood, the police were already there.

Imani wanted to feel conned. It was Ms. Wheeler, after all, who'd led her to believe that betraying Diego's trust was the fit course of action. But as consoling as this thought was, a surge of honesty prevented her from blaming Ms. Wheeler. The scheme had been *Imani's* idea. And, for all she knew, Ms. Wheeler was right. All of her actions leading up to that moment might have been the model of fitness. Maybe it was this belated crisis of conscience that would doom her in the end. She was supposed to have faith in the score and in the five elements of fitness. Hadn't Imani learned this from the example of Ms. Wheeler and the other high 90s? Would Anil Hanesh be standing at the edge of Marina Road trying to reverse his actions for the benefit of an *unscored*? What was Diego Landis anyway but another gum wrapper to be discarded?

The wind blew down the Causeway, and Imani tucked farther into the marsh reeds, wanting to dissolve into the muck and tang of her beloved wetlands. She'd had such big dreams. She was going to be the savior of Somerton, cruising down the river with her fancy degree and her specialized knowledge, the secrets of life itself instilled, through hours of research, into the folds of her brain. Now look at her. She was even less than those stone creatures across the street. At least they had never abandoned a friend or betrayed a trust.

For a long time, Imani sat rubbing her cell's tap screen against her thigh and watching the time progress by minutes, until a sound in the distance roused her. At first, she thought it was a flock of geese, but as it approached, recognition made her heart race. She stood up and went to the edge of Marina Road, holding her breath in anticipation.

A few seconds later, Frankenscooter crested the hill.

Bending low over the handlebars, and charging at breakneck speed, Cady rounded the 7-Eleven. Imani readied herself to dodge as Cady veered toward her, and was still in that readied posture as Cady fishtailed to a halt only inches from her knees. Cady threw Imani her helmet, then lifted the visor on her own.

"Cell died," she said. "We're going to have to break some speed limits."

Imani stuffed her head into her helmet and climbed on. "Whatever it takes," she said.

With a lurch and a fishtail, they were off.

19. the free fall café

THERE WERE ONLY a few cars on the Causeway, but Cady enraged them all as she weaved, bobbed, and ran red lights. The eyeballs ticked by overhead. Imani knew her score was plummeting, and, though she could feel the weight of it in the pit of her stomach, her mind blazed with a single purpose: to save Diego Landis.

In nearly impossible time, they arrived at the wrought iron archway of St. James College.

"Where to?" Cady shouted.

"Abate Hall," Imani said. "But I don't know where that is."

"I do."

Cady sped up and cut diagonally across a quad whose velvety lawn yielded muddily to Frankenscooter's all-terrain tires. The campus was like something from another world, with dignified stone buildings standing next to modern glass ones, and in between, a lush landscaping that Imani knew was maintained by people like her parents: townies, locals, clamdiggers. The university was one of the biggest employers in Somerton, in need of a steady supply of janitors, maids, gardeners, and food servers.

Cady drove past a cathedral, then came to a sudden halt at a bike rack in front of an old stone building.

"I'm pretty sure this is it," Cady said. "Student Center or something?"

The words Anthony Abate Hall were carved into the stone facade. Parked right in front were four police cruisers.

Imani gave Cady her helmet and started up the broad stone steps. "Wait here for me," she said.

"No way," Cady said, stowing their helmets and racing to catch up with Imani.

A pair of college students looked at them curiously from where they sat smoking cigarettes on the steps.

Inside the entrance, beneath a stone archway, was a huge corkboard layered with announcements, in the center of which was a postcard-sized flyer for the Chaos Foundation, which read:

Free Fall Café 10 p.m. Wednesday

"I think that's the pub upstairs," Cady said. "Come on."

Imani followed her up a wide spiral staircase. "How do you know this?"

"Parker's cousin comes to parties here all the time," she said. "Did you hear that?"

It sounded like the pop and squeal of a PA system. Imani and Cady followed it to the second floor. At the entrance to the Free Fall Café, two alarming sights greeted them. The first was a deconstructed eyeball nailed above the entrance, its innards splayed out like a squid autopsy. The second was a group of Somerton police officers facing what looked like a small stage.

The pub was packed with college students, so Imani's view of the stage was obstructed, but she could just make out the girl with the black-and-white hair holding a microphone with something strapped across her chest. "I'd like to thank Somerton's finest for joining us," she sneered into the mike.

The crowd hooted and cheered while the cops, some of them no older than the students, shuffled nervously. Imani recognized an 80 among them who'd graduated from Somerton High three years earlier, but couldn't remember his name. His blue police hat dwarfed his long lean face. She took Cady's hand and cut through a group of college guys toward the stage.

"Look," one of them said. "Townies."

The stage was totally blocked by police and students, some of whom stood on chairs chanting "Police state!"

"So this is illegal now?" the girl shouted into the mike.

Gripping Cady's hand, Imani pushed between two clusters of students until she could see a sliver of the stage. Diego stood there toward the back, looking down at something in his hands.

"I can't see anything," Cady shouted over the growing chants.

There was a low rumbling from somewhere, and the cops who were still blocking most of the stage started fidgeting with their hands on the butts of their pistols.

"All right," the black-and-white-haired girl said. "Let's do it."

Imani tensed, pulling Cady close to her.

A terrible screech emanated from the stage, followed by a low *boom boom boom!*

Imani braced for gunfire or a stampede to the exits, but the cops didn't move. The chants of "Police state!" began to fade as she realized that someone was playing music. Loud, peculiar music.

When two cops faced each other to yell into each other's ears, a sliver of the stage became visible again. This time, Imani could see Diego better. He had his head bent over the neck of a bass guitar. At his side, the girl played a distorted guitar riff while singing nonsense syllables into the microphone. Imani pushed her way between the two cops, pulling Cady after her. Behind a drum kit at the back of the stage, a guy with a shaved head beat out an irregular rhythm.

Cady plastered her mouth to Imani's ear. "*This* is the Chaos Foundation?"

Never in her life had Imani felt stupider than she did at that moment.

"It's a *band*?" Cady asked.

A great mushroom cloud of embarrassment engulfed Imani

as she watched the trio play their music. Diego Landis was a bass player. *Not* a dangerous radical plotting subversive acts. He was a musician, a guy in a band. The ordinariness of it, the sheer *harmlessness* of it, stunned her.

When the first song ended, the crowd cheered and whistled, then half of them headed for the exits, drawn, Imani figured, by the potential for police action more than by the band itself. The police conferred among themselves for a moment, then they too left.

No one was arrested.

Cady tugged on Imani's arm and asked what they should do. The sting of Imani's stupidity had yet to subside, but there was one consolation: the fact that Ms. Wheeler, because she was the one who actually called the police, would look even stupider.

Imani grinned in spite of herself. "Can we sit for a minute?" she asked.

Cady nodded, and they took two seats in the back. With the crowd thinned to a few dozen, they had a good view of the stage, where the trio had begun another song.

The Chaos Foundation was not a band in the same sense that, say, the Beatles were a band. They didn't play songs you'd dance or hum along to. To Imani, it sounded more like traffic than music. Cady tried to immerse herself in it, bobbing her head along with the beat, but as soon as a rhythm was established, the drummer, obeying their defining ethos, would veer into new avenues of chaos.

"Nobody's dancing," Cady said. "Is that a bad sign? Do you *like* this?"

Imani couldn't say whether she liked or disliked the music. It seemed beyond her. But she didn't want to leave, and, after a while, she found herself focusing entirely on Diego, picking out the deep rumble and *phwaatt* of his bass against the wall of noise. His white shirt was rolled up past his elbows, and the sinewy muscles of his right arm pulsed with his plucking. His head was lowered over the instrument, dark hair swaying, eyes closed. Imani had never seen him so unguarded.

"You're staring." Cady's hand fell in an arc in front of Imani's face.

Imani sat upright and forced herself to look at the drummer instead.

When the song ended, Diego twisted the tuning pegs while squinting against the spotlight into the sparse crowd.

"He *is* cute," Cady said.

Imani shrugged.

When the Chaos Foundation began another, quieter song, Cady scooted her chair right up to Imani's. "So I have to ask. Did you . . ." She bit her lip. "Did you watch the . . ."

"The footage?"

Cady's tiny features puckered into a cringe. "God, I hate that word."

"Me too," Imani said. "Of course I didn't watch it."

Cady sighed. "I didn't think you would. But thanks."

It had been harder to resist than Cady probably realized. There was so much Imani wanted to know. Was it worth it? Was it wonderful? Did it hurt? Did Cady still love Parker?

"So what now?" Cady asked.

Imani shook her head. Less than a week remained before her final score was in, enough time to minimize the damage, perhaps, but no more than that. She tried to picture the numbers on that sheet of paper Mrs. Bronson would tape to the glass wall. Fifty-two? Forty-two? Lower? Is that what she was now? A bona fide lowbie?

"Are you all right?" Cady asked.

Imani realized she'd shuddered. "Do you ever wonder who you are?" she asked. "I mean, do you ever think you don't know anymore?"

Cady inclined her head at Imani, a pose of authority undermined by her size relative to Imani and her adorable features. "*I* know who you are," she said.

"Yeah," Imani answered. "You do, don't you?"

The song ended, and the singer thanked the crowd, the members of which were already heading to the bar.

"He just saw you," Cady said. She motioned with her head to the stage, where Diego watched Imani while winding a cable. "Should I go to the bar or something?" Cady asked.

"I don't know," Imani said. "I'm not sure what to say to him."

"Well, he's coming over, so think quick." Cady extricated herself from the chair and went to the bar.

Diego arrived a few seconds later, his bass guitar slung over his shoulder. "You came."

"Well, you were right," Imani said. "Words could not have described that." *Although,* she thought, *they would have been awfully helpful.*

Diego slumped slightly. "You hated it," he said.

"No," Imani said. "I don't think I'm qualified to hate it. I didn't *get* it."

Diego leaned his bass guitar against the table and sat down. "I've been told we're an acquired taste."

"Like bluefish?" Imani asked brightly.

"Yeah," he said doubtfully. "Like bluefish." He twisted around to look at the bar, where Cady sat alone drinking a ginger ale. "Did you come here with Cady Fazio?"

"Yup."

Cady waved nervously at him, and he waved back.

"Isn't that bad for your score?" he asked.

"Yup."

Diego looked at her searchingly, and Imani realized she'd become unfathomable to him again.

"Diego," she said, "can I ask you a question?"

"Sure."

"Are you a spy?"

Diego's eyes widened.

"Is that why your parents enrolled you at Somerton High?" she asked. "So you could spy on Ms. Wheeler?"

He looked like he'd just been ambushed, and for a moment Imani dared to hope that his answer would be yes. It would make it so much easier to confess her betrayal if he did it first.

"You're actually being serious right now, aren't you?" he said. "You're honestly asking me if I'm"—he paused to parse the concept, as if he could only consider it in sections—"a *spy?*"

Imani sucked in air through her teeth. "So you're not?" she said.

"Why on earth would I spy on Ms. Wheeler?" he asked.

Imani deflated quickly. She glanced at Cady, who was staring at her over the lip of her glass. "I'll be right back," she said. Imani rose to leave, but Diego put his hand over hers and anchored it to the table. Imani froze, half out of her chair.

"What's going on?" he asked.

"Nothing," she said. She stared at his hand, too nervous to move. "I was just, um, curious about why, you know, with your family's money, you weren't at a private school or something. But it doesn't matter."

Diego let go of her hand and settled back in his chair. "Okay, look," he said. "I was thrown out of Benford Arts Academy for completely bogus reasons."

"*What?*" Imani sat back down in her chair. "You were *thrown out* of another school?"

Diego looked to the side for a moment to compose himself. "I have a small problem with authority," he said. "Which *some people* consider a weakness."

"Thrown out?" Imani repeated. "Like expelled?"

Diego nodded. "My parents decided they weren't going to spend any more money on private schools, so they told me I'd have to finish out at Somerton."

"As punishment," Imani said, her mood darkening.

"Actually, I prefer it to the private schools I went to," he said. "It's weird, but I like being around so many scored kids. I don't have to worry about fitting in. I'm an automatic outcast."

Imani stared at him.

"What?" he said. "I'm not saying I *like* the scored. But it's better than hanging around a bunch of overprivileged rich kids." He closed his eyes for a second. "And yes, I know I'm an overprivileged rich kid too. So please don't feel the need to remind me."

Imani was flabbergasted by this turn of events. Every time she discovered something about Diego, he revealed another layer.

"Did Ms. Wheeler know this about you when you arrived?" she asked.

"Are you kidding?" he asked. "She tried to use it to keep me out. She has a personal grudge against my mother. A lot of people do." Diego rolled his eyes. "It's a *huge* pain in the ass having a semi-famous mother. Sometimes I wish she'd just go back to corporate law."

"Wait," Imani said. "Aren't you involved in her work?"

Diego snorted. "Uh, thanks but no thanks," he said.

"You're not?" Imani was stupefied.

"Don't get me wrong," he said. "I totally respect what she's doing. But me? I just want to graduate, play my music, and see where life takes me. I am in no way interested in *politics*." He spat out the word as if it were a bug that had flown into his mouth.

Imani stared at him. "But you're so political in class!" she insisted. "You're *belligerent*."

"I know." He grinned at her. "It's fun, isn't it? Especially with you there. Your nose wrinkles in this amazingly cute way when you're upset, like–*there*." He pointed at her nose. "You're doing it right now."

Imani's hand went to her nose.

"I love that," he said.

Imani held his teasing gaze for a while, then turned away.

"Why do you always do that?" he asked.

"Do what?"

"Look away," he said. "You always look away just when it's getting interesting."

She faced him now, and he wasn't grinning anymore. He looked nervous. "Did you really come here for the music?" he asked.

Imani shook her head.

Diego smiled. "I didn't think so."

"Diego—"

"It's okay," he said. "I didn't invite you here for the music."

"Diego, really—"

"Just—" He held up his hand to stop her. Then his voice fell to a whisper. "Just keep looking at me."

Imani did keep looking at him, wondering if her nose was doing that thing he loved. She could see his chest rise and fall in nervous breaths and knew hers was rising and falling too. How, she wondered, had they wound up *here*? She'd shown him nothing but contempt, heaping doses of it. Now he was looking at her the way Malachi Beene once had.

"How many days until your final score?" he asked.

"Diego—"

"I can wait," he said. "I wouldn't want to make things worse for you."

His blue eye locked on hers, and she had to force herself to look away.

"I'll be right back," she said. Before he could protest, she went to the bar, where Cady, slurping the remains of her ginger ale, gaped at her in animated query. Imani calmly removed a napkin from the dispenser and asked to borrow the bartender's pen. When she returned to Diego, she wrote her phone number on the napkin and slid it to him. Then, before he could misinterpret its intent, she gave him his instructions.

"Tell your mother to call me first thing in the morning."

"My *mother*?"

"Yes," Imani said. She kept her tone businesslike. "I have information about Ms. Wheeler that could help her."

Diego stared at her, puzzled.

"And I'm sorry," she said.

Diego looked at the napkin, then back at her. "What are you sorry for?"

Imani forced herself to remain cool, detached. "I'm sorry for tomorrow," she said.

She motioned for Cady to follow her to the exit. She never looked back at Diego.

20. something like friends

DIEGO'S MOTHER CALLED at six the next morning, waking Imani from a deep sleep.

"My son says you have information for me?" she said. Her tone was cautious, skeptical.

Imani had gone to bed the previous night convinced that a full confession was in order, and that she would never have the courage to make that confession to Diego. But now that his mother was on the other end of the phone, she began to doubt herself.

"What exactly is the nature of your association with Ms. Wheeler?" Mrs. Landis asked.

Imani laughed nervously. "Well, that's kind of the problem," she said. Then she began her tale. About one minute into it, Mrs. Landis interrupted to ask if she could record it.

"Why?" Imani asked.

Mrs. Landis laughed lightheartedly. "I'm useless with note-taking," she said. "My hand has already cramped up. Do you mind?"

"Um, I guess not," Imani said. Then she told her the rest of the story.

When she had finished, Mrs. Landis paused before speaking. "Are you saying that Ms. Wheeler told you this would *help* your score?"

"At first, she said it was uncharted territory," Imani explained. "But then yesterday, she told me she was sure I'd get over the scholarship line because of it."

"You realize that's a lie, of course."

Imani's heart sank, which she knew was absurd. Imani hadn't believed Ms. Wheeler when she'd said it, and, at any rate, she had done so much to destroy her score between then and now that it shouldn't have mattered. But hope could be so stubborn. Even false, deluded hope. "I figured it was a lie," she said.

"Okay then," Mrs. Landis said. "Is there anything else?"

"No. That's all."

"Will I see you at the meeting tonight?"

"I don't think so," Imani said.

"Okay. I do appreciate your candor," Mrs. Landis said. "You did the right thing."

"Did I?"

"Yes," Mrs. Landis said. "Belatedly, but yes."

After Imani hung up, she sat on her bed staring through the

window as the sky brightened with the morning. Her confession did not, as she had hoped, lighten her load. If anything, she felt heavier.

Imani arrived at American history class early that day, took her usual seat, and began slow deep breaths in anticipation of Diego's arrival. She presumed that Mrs. Landis had told him the whole story but was holding out hope—false, deluded hope, perhaps—that she hadn't. Imani had already decided not to look at him in class, because no mere glance could make amends for what she had done.

Students drifted in one by one. Even Mr. Carol arrived on time. It was only when the late bell rang and Mr. Carol sat on the middle desk that Imani realized Diego wasn't coming. That meant he knew. His mother had told him and he was so angry that he couldn't bear the sight of her.

The topic of the day, ironically, was civility in dissent. While Mr. Carol lectured them on how reasonable people could disagree without resorting to character assassination or accusations of stupidity, Imani glanced repeatedly at Diego's empty chair. She knew he would return to school before long. Pride, if nothing else, would force him to face her. But no matter how eloquently he argued in class, Imani knew she'd miss their private disagreements. Despite his defects, Diego, in all fairness, had a mind to be reckoned with. She realized how much she would have enjoyed cowriting that essay with him, now that it was no longer a possibility. If she hadn't spoiled things with her appalling betrayal, and he hadn't spoiled things with his confession of feelings, perhaps, she thought, after her final score was in, they might have become something like friends. Now they'd never know.

For the rest of the day, Imani wandered through the hallways and endured her classes as if in a daze. Her teachers' voices were an irrelevant drone, and her fellow students had become universally distasteful to her—both the lowbies and the highbies, but especially the highbies. She no longer envied them. They seemed lifeless, inhuman. What she wanted, more than she'd ever wanted it before, was to be on the river. So, for the second day in a row, Imani decided to cut school early. On her way to the exit, she passed Deon, hugging a chemistry book while avoiding eye contact with everyone. As she watched him shuffle meekly to class, she realized there was one last thing to do before she left.

She went to the school library, waited for a tablet to become available, then printed out the article Diego had shown her from *Neuroscience Quarterly*. When the bell rang, she found Deon at his locker. He shrunk from her approach, but Imani was not there to attempt friendship; she was there to help him escape. She told him about Amber's plan to ostracize him from the gang, and, since she knew Deon would have no idea what to do with such information, she handed him the article she'd printed.

"The gangs are a bug, not a feature," she explained, while flipping to the page she'd highlighted. "You don't have to sit with the sixties at lunch just because you're a sixty. It doesn't help you. It might even prevent you from ascending."

"But where would I sit?" he asked, without looking at her.

"You could sit alone if you wanted," she said.

He looked up from the article, suddenly hopeful.

"You're under no obligation to the sixties, Deon. You get no advantage from them. And they're about to dump you. Why not dump them first?"

Deon looked down and speed-read the section Imani had highlighted.

"You can keep that," Imani said.

Then she left him alone, which she knew was his preference.

Imani took the river at breakneck speed, heading straight for Hogg Island with her clam fork and bag. In the Corona Point channel, her motor started clicking oddly, so she pulled into the small strip of beach by the abandoned marina. She lifted the motor out of the water to have a look but could find nothing awry.

Not far away were the cliff steps that led to Diego's house. She wondered if he was there now or if he was out tearing up the dunes on his scooter. She tried to imagine what Diego did when he felt the way *she* felt. Then she realized he wouldn't feel the way she felt. Whatever state of lousiness he was in would be complementary to hers, not identical.

She dropped the motor back in the water and, not wanting to risk getting stranded on Hogg Island, went home.

As she approached the marina, her father, hearing her boat, looked up from the drainage pump of the Lowries' whaler. He walked down to the slip to meet her, wiping his hands on the front of his jeans. "Your mother says you cut school early?" he called out to her.

Imani tied up Frankenwhaler and lifted the motor out of the water. "I think there's something up with Cady's board. Can you look at it?"

"Not answering my questions anymore?" Mr. LeMonde stood rigid on the dock, pointedly refusing to look at Imani's motor.

"I didn't feel well," she said defensively.

"But you had a miraculous recovery, I see."

"Dad—" Imani looked away, to the remnants of Frankenwhaler's wake lapping the muddy edges of the marina.

Her father stood still for a moment, waiting for Imani to change her mind and talk to him. When she didn't, he climbed into her boat with a little groan. "Let's have a look, then." He opened a compartment in the motor and poked around. "Yup," he said. "Wrong screws." He held one up for Imani to see. "Cady is all about power, but she's impatient with the details. You can't go sticking these things in willy-nilly."

"And I paid her in lobster."

Imani sat on the edge of the boat and watched him carefully remove the rest of the screws, wishing she'd spent as much time learning from him about motors as Cady had. They'd have had so much more to talk about then. But Score Corp had identified her core strengths as academic, not technical, and Imani had gone along with it. She'd never even questioned it.

"Hey, Dad," she said. "Do you have to go to Isiah's scrimmage tonight? Could Mom go instead?"

"Why?" He pulled the circuit board out.

"Because I was wondering if you'd go to that meeting with me," she asked nervously.

"So you *do* think the LeMondes should be represented."

Imani looked down and laughed nervously. "Oh, I have a feeling we'll be represented, all right."

Her father shifted his weight. "Imani Jane, what have you gone and done?"

When she looked up at him, she almost told him the truth. But there was too much to tell, and she wasn't ready yet. "Will you go with me?" she asked coyly.

After a moment, her father took her hand and helped her out of the boat. "Could I say no to my one and only daughter?"

They headed down the dock together.

"Hey, Dad, did you ever read the book *Brave New World* in high school?"

"Sounds familiar," he said. "I think it was assigned. But unless it was a comic book or a dirty magazine, I probably didn't read it."

If Elon LeMonde had been scored as a teenager, he would have undoubtedly been a lowbie.

21. undertow

THE AUDITORIUM WAS standing room only. Up by the stage, Ms. Wheeler huddled with members of the town council, her crisp pink suit expressing a soft nurturing approachability backed by a spine of pure steel. She appeared unaffected by the mishap at St. James College and showed no sign of knowing that Imani had ratted her out to Mrs. Landis. But the calm she exuded seemed forced to Imani, who could see in her the Wakachee teenager she'd once been—ambitious, tightly controlled, but intensely aware of the possibility of total failure. Despite all that had transpired between them, Imani couldn't help but feel sorry for her.

Imani stood with her father in the back, unsure of what her role would be. But whereas her father had an air of cautious excitement about the proceedings, Imani was all sharp nerves.

Scanning the auditorium, she spotted Cady and Parker. They stood behind a tall slender woman Imani recognized instantly as Diego's mother. They had the same piercing eyes, the same straight dark hair. Seeing Cady wave to Imani, Mrs. Landis made her way through the crowd and introduced herself.

"I'm glad you're here, Imani," she said. She turned to Imani's father. "You must be—"

"Elon LeMonde," he said, shaking her hand.

"You should be very proud of your daughter," Mrs. Landis said.

"Is that so?" Mr. LeMonde looked at Imani pointedly.

Catching on to his ignorance of the activities in question, Mrs. Landis changed the subject. "I was wondering, Imani. How would you feel about speaking tonight?"

"You mean live? In front of all these people?"

"All you'd have to do is answer some questions. It's up to you."

Imani could feel the blood draining from her face.

"Okay," Mrs. Landis said in an accommodating tone. "Alternatively, I could play the recording of our phone conversation. Would that be better?"

"Imani?" her father said. "At some point are you going to tell me what's going on?"

Imani looked from her father to Mrs. Landis, both of whom wanted different things from her and wanted them badly.

"I don't want to put any pressure on you," Mrs. Landis said. "I know you've already been through a lot, but don't you think the people of Somerton have a right to know who their school principal is?"

It could ruin her, Imani thought.

Mrs. Landis leaned in and spoke softly. "She won't stop, you know. She won't give up until every unscored is banned from this school. Do you think that's right, Imani?"

Mrs. Landis was so sure of herself, Imani thought, so firm in her convictions. She was, in a way, just like Ms. Wheeler.

"Look," Mrs. Landis said. "I don't want to stress, but—"

"Play it," Imani said. "It's the truth. Play it."

"Now, hold on," Mr. LeMonde said, holding out his hands. "What exactly are we talking about here, Imani?"

"Play it," Imani said.

"Okay," Mrs. Landis said. "Why don't we do this. I've got the recording. When I go up to speak tonight, if you want to join me, just head down to the front of the auditorium. No pressure. How's that?"

"I won't be speaking," Imani said.

"Either way," Mrs. Landis said, "I want you to know you're a brave girl."

Imani nodded noncommittally. Brave was the last thing she felt. She supposed Mrs. Landis meant that it had taken courage to come clean about her actions, but it was the kind of thing only someone with firm convictions would say. What Mrs. Landis didn't seem to realize was that Imani's convictions were anything but firm. She had gotten there by riding an undertow of half-buried feelings that didn't quite rise to the level of conviction. It was that pull—possibly familial, possibly even genetic—that had delivered her there. It wasn't bravery. It was more like surrender.

When Mrs. Landis returned to Cady and Parker and a clutch of other people who all seemed to work for her, Imani began to feel as if the whole enterprise was as muddled as she was. And that it was missing the point.

There was a small commotion at the door, then Diego pushed his way through. A few underclassman highbies parted for him with eyes averted. He stood behind the last row of chairs.

Imani watched him, then gripped her father's hand.

"Who's that?" her father asked, looking at Diego.

Diego hadn't spotted her yet, but as he scanned the auditorium, Imani's throat went dry.

"My victim," she said hoarsely.

"Imani?" her father asked.

"Don't worry, Dad," she said. "You're about to find out everything."

Up on the stage, Ms. Wheeler walked to the podium. "Wow," she said. "What a great turnout. Those of you in back, there are a few chairs up front here."

Two parents standing next to Diego brushed past him to claim those chairs. Diego turned and saw Imani, locked his eye on hers for a moment, then turned coldly away.

Ms. Wheeler began her speech, but Imani could barely take it in, something about "tough choices" and "brighter futures for everyone's children." Imani was staring at Diego's profile, willing him to look at her. His long hair obscured his face, but Imani was certain he could feel her presence.

Ms. Wheeler was making a brilliant case. The unscored were "spoilers," who prevented the score from "fulfilling its promise" of upward mobility and true meritocracy. Though she no longer had the trump card of Diego's arrest to boost her case, Imani knew she'd win people over.

Imani began a mental countdown. Ms. Wheeler was savvy. She would be persuasive but concise. She wouldn't risk boring her audience with a surplus of detail. It would be so much more expedient to feed their fear with a few indisputable facts, then leave them to imagine the horrors of inaction on their own. Then she'd step down and Mrs. Landis would take the stage. At that point, Imani's actions would be known by everybody. Nicknames would be thought up for her. Irrelevant but plausible-seeming sexual connotations inferred. She was, after all, the best friend of Cady Fazio, the star of Farm Field F *& k Fest. The episode of Imani LeMonde, Ad Hoc Spy, would seep through all elements of Somerton society, leaving a residue of shame and self-righteousness whose most enduring impact would be to fuel the system that had given rise to it in the first place. The system was robust, she realized, and could turn any-thing to the cause of its own survival. And this show, Imani conjectured, this contest between Patrina Wheeler and Dena Landis, meant nothing.

In the end, Score Corp would win.

Imani could sense Ms. Wheeler nearing the end of her argument. In moments, Mrs. Landis would take the stage and make Imani's secret transgressions public. She probably deserved what was coming, and, for a moment, she entertained the pos-sibility that such an extreme and public undoing would leave her cleansed. But something gnawed at her.

"Dad," she said, "I have to go do something. Will you wait for me here?"

"What?" he whispered. "Where are you going?"

"Trust me?" Imani said.

"Imani Jane!" he whispered.

"Please?"

Her father took a moment to consider, then, perhaps suspecting that she was more her father's daughter than either of them had realized, he nodded his ascent. Imani went to the double doors where Diego stood.

"Walk with me?" she said.

He didn't answer, but when she left the auditorium, he waited a few seconds, then followed. As Imani made her way down the hallway, he stayed at least ten feet behind, a move designed to fool the eyeballs.

Imani wanted to be alone with him, but the hallways were dotted with Somerton police patrolling for troublemakers. Eventually, she arrived at Mr. Carol's classroom, which was left unlocked. Imani opened the door, waited for Diego to turn the corner and see her, then went inside. The second hand swept from the eight to the ten before Diego entered and closed the door.

It was dim in the classroom, possibly too dim for the eyeball to identify her, possibly not.

"What do you want?" he asked.

"How much do you know?"

"Everything you told my mother."

It was a lot, but it wasn't everything.

"Did you bring me here to apologize?" he asked. "Because it's not necessary."

"Does that mean you've forgiven me?"

"No," he said. "I'm skipping forgive. I'm going right to forget. Can I repeat my first question? What do you want?"

The desks still sat in their loose circle, split down the middle. Imani leaned against one on the unscored half.

"Look," Diego said. "I really don't need an explanation for what you did. It's pretty obvious, so you can save the–"

Imani shut him up by kissing him. She was so fast off her desk, he had no time to prepare. She'd only grazed his lips when he pulled away and fixed her with an accusing glare. "What is wrong with you?" he asked.

"I don't know," she said. "Everything?"

Diego closed his eyes and tilted his head back. "Is it your aim in life to toy with me, Imani?"

"No."

He looked at her, breathing heavily. "Because I'm really in no mood to be–"

She shut him up again. This time, he surrendered immediately. When their lips separated, they remained so close Imani could barely focus on him. His arms had found her waist, and Imani was resting her wrists on his shoulders. The warmth of him made her dizzy, and all she wanted was to dive back into that blurry miasma of feeling and want.

But something drew her attention. Behind Diego, the eyeball dangled. It was the same eyeball she'd seen every day in American history. It was exactly like every other eyeball in the world. Pulling free of Diego, she went and stood underneath it, the fabric of the American flag grazing her shoulder.

"Um, Imani?" he said. "You're not about to do one of those eyeball confessions, are you?"

"Hmm?" She was mesmerized by the shiny black face, as if seeing it for the first time.

"Because I think that might freak me out," Diego said.

So small, she thought, *so shiny, like a Christmas ornament.* She grabbed the flagpole in both hands and yanked it out of its stand.

"Imani, what are you doing?" Diego's voice had taken on the tone of a concerned teacher.

But she was under the sway of something powerful, something deep and, while not identifiable, not entirely unknown. Swinging the flagpole behind her, she touched its tip to the floor. Then, aiming carefully, she swung upward as if at a tiny piñata. With a crash and a tinkle, the eyeball shattered.

"Oh my God," Diego said behind her.

Calmly, Imani returned the flagpole to its holder, then stood and watched as the remains of the eyeball, a half dome now, swung back and forth, its circuitry dangling like entrails. Diego picked his way over the bits of glass and stood next to her to watch it swing, first in wide arcs, then medium, then small.

"I don't even know what to say," he whispered.

"Then don't say anything."

He looked right at her, and this time she didn't look away.

Outside the classroom, the noise was growing—Ms. Wheeler, Mrs. Landis, cheering, booing, police shuffling, then running, through the hallways. The meeting was descending into chaos. Imani knew she should have been there to answer for her actions and to stand up for what she believed in. But what did she believe in? Her beliefs had been programmed into her, designed to shape her into the fittest person she could become. In the end, the only beliefs that remained were the ones that were dooming her. So she stayed with Diego in Mr. Carol's dimly lit classroom.

"Hey, do you want to go clamming with me on Saturday?" she asked.

"Uh, sure," he said. "But you'll have to teach me. I've never even held a clam fork."

Imani shook her head.

"Well, I bet you've never held a bass guitar," he said, only slightly miffed.

"True," she said. Then she smiled coyly. "Are you proposing a discreet collaboration?"

Diego stepped forward and took one of her hands. "I don't know, Imani. Look where the last one got us." Their eyes drifted to the broken eyeball still swinging in barely perceptible arcs.

"I'm game if you are," she said. Then she took his other hand and looked into the piercing blue eye that had once intimidated her. If this was doom, she thought, she'd take it.

"Oh, I'm game," he said. He leaned forward and kissed her.

In the moment before Imani closed her eyes to get lost in that kiss, she noticed that the broken eyeball had stopped swinging at last.

THE OTIS INSTITUTE
INNOVATION IN EDUCATION

Dear Ms. LeMonde and Mr. Landis:

It is with great pleasure that we offer you a scholarship in the amount of $40,000, to be divided as you see fit. Furthermore, we would like to extend our congratulations on a fine essay. Your mutual insights on individualism and camaraderie were most enlightening. We wish you both the best of luck in your academic endeavors and look forward to hearing about your accomplishments in the years to come.

Sincerely,

Kathleen Otis

Kathleen Otis
Director, The Otis Institute

acknowledgments

Thanks to Dad for all those summers on the boat, and to Lufkin Marina for the memories. Thanks to my early readers (Mom, Dad, Andrew, Scott, and Justine) for pointing out what should probably have been obvious but wasn't. Thanks to my agent, Jill Grinberg, for always knowing what's best, and to my editor, Mallory Lochr, for challenging me.

lauren mclaughlin

grew up in the small town of Wenham, Massachusetts. After college and a brief stint in graduate school, she spent ten "unglamorous" years writing and producing movies before abandoning her screen ambitions to write fiction full-time. Though she fondly remembers much of her time in Massachusetts—the marina, the beach, various teenage escapades—she cannot, for the life of her, remember her SAT scores, her GPA, or any of the numbers that once summed her up.